# The
# WEDDING
# DRESS

*The*

# WEDDING

# DRESS

~~~

## GARY E. PARKER

*Run So That You May Win*
iVictor.com

Victor is an imprint of
Cook Communications Ministries, Colorado Springs, Colorado 80918
Cook Communications, Paris, Ontario
Kingsway Communications, Eastbourne, England

THE WEDDING DRESS
© 2001 by Gary E. Parker

First Printing, 2001
Printed in Singapore by Tien Wah Press Pte Ltd
1 2 3 4 5 6 7 8 9 10 Printing/Year 05 04 03 02 01

Editor: Craig Bubeck, Sr. Editor
Cover Design: Andrea L. Boven / Boven Design Studio
Cover Photograph: Brad Armstrong Photography
Interior Design: Andrea L. Boven / Boven Design Studio

**Library of Congress Cataloging-in-Publication Data**

Parker, Gary E.
    The wedding dress / Gary E. Parker.
      p. cm.
    ISBN 0-78143-700-8
    1. Adult children of aging parents--Fiction.  2. Alzheimer's
disease--Patients--Fiction.  3. Mothers and daughters--Fiction.  I.
Title.
  PS3566.A6784 W43 2002
  813'.54--dc21

                                    2001005276

# Table of Contents

*God will not look you over for*

*medals, degrees or diplomas,*

*but for scars.*

ELBERT HUBBARD

ᴏᴄ♥ᴄᴏ

# *Decisions*

BRAKING HER FOUR-YEAR-OLD PICK-UP TO A QUICK STOP, RACHEL
Lewis pushed out of the seat, pulled her tan suit jacket tight to
keep off the misty rain, and hustled across the yard of
Momma's two-story white-framed house. Fronted by a stand of
eight oaks, the house had seen a hundred years come and go.
A porch wrapped all the way across the front and down the
right side, and a thick blanket of ivy clutched the chimney on
the left. Two rocking chairs sat on the porch, though no one
had rocked in them for at least a year. Indeed, the chairs—like
the house—needed painting.

At the door, Rachel squared her shoulders and assured herself once more that she had no choice in what she had come to
do. Life didn't always bring easy options; and today of all
days—Mother's Day—she had to face one of the hardest that a
son or daughter could ever bump up against. She might as
well do it fast—put the awful deed in the rear view mirror and
move on.

The front door creaked as she pushed through it, and the
distinct smell of a house where the windows have been a long-
-time closed rushed over her. She wrinkled her nose and made
a mental note to give the place a thorough cleaning as soon as
possible. "Scrub it like a granny woman," she whispered. She

began formulating an agenda: mop the hardwood floors; wash, dry and iron the draperies; brush the cobwebs out of every corner in the ten rooms; and take a steel wool pad to all the sinks and bathrooms. Make the house spic and span, so clean it would almost seem that . . .

Rachel smiled ruefully as she recognized that she was focusing on chores in order to distract herself from a heavy burden. She did that a lot. But this time, no matter how hard she scrubbed, she didn't think she could remove the stains left by the memories of the last six years. Those stains were as dyed into her soul like red on an apple.

"Hey, Josey," she called loudly, pushing away the unpleasant.

"In here," Josey yelled from the rear of the house. "With your Momma."

Rachel brushed her hands on the front of her navy slacks. She needed to hurry, no doubt about it. But her feet felt glued to the floor. She glanced down. Baby-doll feet, her husband Tim called them. Barely wide enough to keep a body properly balanced. But the feet matched her body—so small that she shopped in the junior section in the department store when she traveled to Hendersonville to buy clothes. Not that she went to Hendersonville that often—no more than three or four times a year. But when she did, well, she bought petite petites and sometimes found even they were too big.

Rachel knew she was stalling, putting off the distasteful task as long as possible. That wasn't like her. At forty-two years old, she hadn't become the top salesperson in the Blue Ridge Realty Company by putting things off. Fact was, folks at BRRC called her "Rush It Rachel" because that's how she was when it came to property appraisals, house mortgages, and settlement lawyers' meetings. One of the new breed of full-time working women of the early 1970s, she believed she had to work twice as hard as a man to achieve anywhere near the same recognition and pay.

But right now Rachel felt powerless to move—as stuck in place as a telephone pole sunk into solid concrete. Taking a deep breath, she took a hard look around the entryway to her childhood home. To her left, a darkly varnished staircase stretched up to the second floor. A glass chandelier—large but not overbearing—hung from the ceiling. The floors were made from oak planks cut from the almost one hundred acres that her family had owned longer than she could begin to remember. An entry hall table with a mirror over it sat on the wall to her left. A rotary phone, the only phone in the house, sat on the table.

Rachel heard feet shuffling from the back of the house. She checked her watch—almost one o'clock. She had an appointment at four with a retired couple from Missouri who wanted to settle in the North Carolina mountains. A sense of urgency pushed up and through her stomach. She had to make it quick if she was going to finish this, go by her house for a minute to see Tim and her twelve-year-old daughter Kara, and still meet the retirees.

Finally forcing herself to move, Rachel passed through the entryway. She saw Josey, her momma's sister and live-in companion for the past five years, moving her heavy body down the hallway. Josey threw up a hand. Rachel hugged hard.

"She's sitting easy," said Josey, stepping past Rachel to the living room and pulling a sweater off the cloth sofa by the window. "Having a pretty good day so far."

Rachel nodded as she followed Josey. With her momma, the good days were rarities to be hoarded as best you could. "She sleep any?" she asked.

"Some, mostly early last night," said Josey, pulling on the sweater, a plain brown thing that struggled to stretch over her broad shoulders. "But not since about four this morning."

Rachel shook her head.

"I've about got things ready for the movers," Josey said. "Best I could anyway."

Rachel looked around the room. By dark tomorrow the house would stand empty. The bedroom suite her stepfather had built for her, from the same oaks as those in the floors, would go into storage in her basement. The table, chairs, buffet, and china cabinet in the dining room where everybody ate after church every Sunday, would go to an antique dealer for sale. Her three step-brothers had claimed several other pieces of the furniture for their families.

"Wish we didn't have to do it," Josey said.

"It's a hard thing," Rachel agreed. "I feel like we're stealing or something, taking Momma's things, scattering them out like leaves in the wind."

"Don't I know it," said Josey, picking her purse off the coffee table. "I ain't got no hankering to do any of this—break up the place, leave Ava and all. But my boy insists. Says I can move down to Greenville to live with him on my own accord, or he's going to strap me to a stretcher and haul me there."

Rachel grinned but only briefly. Her aunt Josey—a widow like her momma—had worn herself out caring for Ava. Rachel knew that an Alzheimer's patient could do that, even to a former nurse like Josey. Thank goodness Josey had arms the size of stove pipes and— until recently—a back strong enough to make an ox jealous.

"Ben is right, you know," said Rachel. "You need to take care of yourself."

"I'm no spring chicken," said Josey. "That's for sure."

For several seconds, the two women faced each other. A ray of sunshine broke through the rectangular windows to Rachel's right, but only for a second. Rachel's heart felt like a lump of coal in her chest. Her aunt Josey, Ava's last living sister, had come down with a back so bad the doctor said she couldn't keep caring for an Alzheimer's patient, no matter how strong the family bond.

"Fact is," said the doctor, "you keep on like you're going, and someone will end up moving in to lift and tote for you."

The news had hit everybody in the family like a brick in the face. Josey took it as a personal insult, the notion that she no longer had what it took to provide for her sister. But everyone had insisted that she listen to the doctor. Then they talked about options for Ava. They could move her into a small house and hire a twenty-four-hour housekeeper to watch over her. They could move her in with one of them. Or one of them could move with family into her house. But, after days of reflection, they saw that none of these solutions made sense. In their corner of the world—a town called Rock Branch with less than five thousand people—they didn't know where to go to hire a live-in helper. And each of them had his or her own families to attend to. It was simply too much to add the burden of their mother to their schedules. Although they all felt guilty about it, they had come to a joint decision about the only other choice available.

Now, remembering the decision, Rachel sensed tears close to
the surface. She moved to Josey and hugged her again. Josey
patted her on the back. "I know child," she soothed.
"Sometimes life is just plain hard."

"I'm so . . . sorry," whispered Rachel. "So . . ."

"Don't you worry none," said Josey. "They will take good
care of your Momma down at Mixon's."

"I just wish . . . I just wish . . ." Her words choked by tears,
Rachel couldn't finish the sentence. Truth was she wished a lot
of things. She wished she didn't have to pack up her momma
today—to move her and a few of her belongings from the
house where she had lived all her life to a nursing home that
promised "Sensitive Care for Special Adults," but smelled like
three-day-old milk. She wished she had the guts to step away
from the real estate business that claimed over fifty hours of
her week. She wished that Kara didn't have to climb off the
bus and go stay with their neighbor Mrs. Becker every afternoon after school. She wished she and Tim still attended blue
grass concerts like they did when they were courting. She
wished she could move her momma into her house and care
for her like she believed a good daughter should.

But none of that was possible. She was "Rush It Rachel," and
who had the time to do all those other things when she had
deals to swing, and appointments to keep, and things to prove,
and . . . goodness, she needed to catch her breath and then get
on with it.

Rachel stepped back from Josey and sucked in her breath.

"I reckon I best go to the store," Josey said softly. "Back in
an hour or so—time for you to get home and see your family
for awhile before you go off to your work."

Rachel nodded. Although Tim had not voiced it—he never did—she knew he disliked her making an appointment on Mother's Day. But she had no control over it. In the real estate business you work when the client wants you, simple as that.

She walked Josey out and watched her drive off in her beat-up station wagon. Then she turned back into the house. By the time Josey returned she would have finished her duty. Ava would sleep tonight in her own house for the last time. The movers would arrive in the morning and haul away her belongings. And Rachel, a real estate agent to the last, would stick a "for sale" sign in the yard, a necessary act so they could pay for Ava's care down at Mixon's. By nightfall tomorrow, her family as she had known it would end. Though Rachel knew she had no choice in moving her momma, she still felt as if someone had reached into her chest with bare hands and pulled out her heart. ❧

# CHAPTER TWO

# *Packing Up*

A STEP INSIDE HER MOMMA'S BEDROOM, AND RACHEL STOPPED, FOLDING her arms across her chest. The first few seconds were always the worst—had been since the doctor first pronounced the chilling judgment "Alzheimer's" almost six years ago. That word had altered Ava's life—and everybody else's around her for that matter—as surely as if someone had taken a hatchet and chopped off one of her arms. Sometimes, even now, that's what it still felt like to Rachel—like someone had amputated something that no one could ever replace.

In some sense, that was true. Alzheimer's had amputated Ava's mind—had removed it with as much precision as the best of surgeons. Only it had taken a lot longer than a typical surgeon who sawed off a body part in one fell swoop. Alzheimer's wasn't nearly so merciful as to do its damage all at once. It operated much more slowly, accomplishing its work in tiny pieces, a snip here and a cut there, a small loss of memory today, a sliver of a bigger one tomorrow.

Rachel dabbed her eyes. A four-poster mahogany bed with a white lace canopy sat in the center of the room. A quilt, hand-stitched with images of summer vegetables, hung over the bed's foot railing, and a simple but elegant white spread lay across it. A tan rug was on the hardwood floor, and a fan that

Ava never used hung from the ceiling. Rachel's eyes moved to the wall behind the bed. Pictures of the family stared back at her—not one or two, but scores of pictures, almost as if her momma had wanted to cover up every speck of the wall with an image of a child or grandchild. About the only person not pictured on the wall was Ava herself.

"I can see me any time I want," Ava would always protest when someone tried to hang a picture that had her in it. "And it ain't that much to look at."

Rachel shook her head. On the point of her own appearance, Ava was less than realistic. In her younger days, Ava compared favorably with any woman in Rock Branch—a movie star look alike with a petite figure, hair the color of cut hay, eyes as blue as a clear mountain sky. She had a face that made you want to smile no matter what your mood.

"She's like walking sunshine," her husband Ray used to say. "A shot of happiness in high heels."

Rachel smiled. Not only did her momma radiate beauty, but she seemed shot with electricity too—a pulsating, active, on-the-go woman. Though no more than five feet five and a hundred and five pounds at her heaviest, Ava had enough energy to put even the hardest laborer to shame. Up by six every morning, she cooked and cleaned and packed school lunches. After herding her children off to school, she drank a quick cup of coffee, rolled up her sleeves, and went right back at it. In the spring she planted a garden, hoed it by hand, picked it and cooked or canned its harvest. When the weather changed and the garden petered out, she took to sewing, sometimes making new clothes, dresses especially, and sometimes repairing old ones. No matter what the season, Ava kept her fingers busy and her mind occupied. If idle hands were the devil's workshop, then the devil never got much work done around Ava. Her only diversions from her chores were her children and her church, and those two mixed so much it was hard to tell where one ended and the other began.

"Your Momma's got more buzz than a bumblebee on sugar water," the preacher at her Methodist church had liked to say. "If I had a dozen of her around here we could bring in the Lord's kingdom in less than a month."

Rachel sighed. The preacher had not said anything like that in a long time. For another second, she stared across the room. As usual, Ava sat in a rocking chair by a pair of rectangular windows, her fingers gripping the rocker's arms as if trying to squeeze the wood into sawdust. She wore a green nightgown and a heavy wool shawl in spite of the fact that a heating vent spewed hot air on her from less than three feet away. A blue blanket lay on her legs. Her hair, silver gray now, fell loose on her shoulders in a wild spray.

Rachel smiled again. Although Ava had not spoken a word in almost a year, she fought like a wet cat when anybody tried to cut or pin back her hair. She would let her or Josey wash and brush it, but if they tried to curl it, cut it, pull it up, or push it back, she squirmed and squealed something fierce. After over a year of such behavior, she and Josey had pretty much given up any hope of changing it.

A clock from the hallway bonged the quarter hour, and Rachel set her chin and moved to Ava. She had a lot to do and not much time to do it—the story of her life.

By the rocker, Rachel bent and kissed her momma on the cheek. Ava glanced up for a second but without recognition.

Her eyes looked like a house somebody had moved out of without turning off the lights.

"You feeling okay today, Momma?" Rachel asked.

Ava didn't offer an answer. Rachel didn't expect one.

"You eat some lunch?" Again, no response.

Rachel adjusted the shawl and pulled the blanket up tighter around her waist. No matter how hot the weather, Ava liked as many blankets as anybody would pile on her. It was almost as if her body heat had ebbed away with her mind.

"Josey went to the grocery store," Rachel said. "She'll come back later."

Ava turned her head and stared out the windows. The earlier mist had transformed into a slow but steady rain. Every now and again thunder rumbled in the distance as a fresh bank of spring clouds rolled past. Water streaked the windows and slithered down the gutters from the roof. It seemed to Rachel that the sky had become as sad as she, but it had given into the desire to cry.

"Everything is blooming," she said, trying to make cheerful conversation. "The roses, columbines, fox glove, everything is real pretty." The rain thumped down even heavier. Lighting zig zagged across the sky. The thunder rocked the floor under Rachel's feet. Her mood sinking even lower, Rachel eased to the corner and pulled a chair close to her momma. Although she knew Ava wouldn't understand a word, she still felt like she owed her an explanation. Sitting down, she took her momma's hands into hers. Ava's eyes stayed focused on something outside, her stare moving past Rachel as if she didn't exist.

Rachel patted Ava's hand. The time had come to say it out loud, maybe for herself more than for her momma. "We're going to move you tomorrow," she said. Ava never blinked. "It's a real nice place about four miles from here," Rachel continued. "You've been there, of course. You used to take apple pies to Betty Buhler when she went in there, after she broke her hip."

Ava licked her lips but otherwise gave no sign of life. But that didn't make Rachel feel any better.

"I'll come see you almost every day," said Rachel. "Won't be much different from now. Just that Josey won't be nearby. And we won't have the house to clean up anymore."

Ava's eyes moved to her hands. She stared at her fingers as if inspecting the world's largest diamond. Rachel wondered for at least the one-millionth time what, if anything, her momma could understand. Were the doctor's right when they said she knew nothing—not where she was, not who she was, not anything?

Rachel had read a lot about Alzheimer's—she knew that it could hit people between the ages of forty and ninety; knew that if one person got it, that increased the odds that a family member would also suffer from it.

She knew the medical explanations too. The neurotransmitters in the brain—the conduits that carry information from one part of the brain to another—get clogged up with sticky clumps of a protein that doctors call "amyloid." He said it was sort of like a water pipe with a clog of hair stopping it up, keeping the water from flushing out. As more and more of these clumps—what doctors label plaques—form, less and less of the brain functions.

At first the person just loses some memory, gets confused, finds normal acts more difficult to achieve. But, as time goes on, the disease makes matters worse and worse. Finally, if the person doesn't die from something else, the Alzheimer's makes him or her unable to do even the simplest things—recognize family members, speak, care for bodily functions. It wasn't a pretty picture; and her momma, though only sixty, was close to the end of the cycle.

Rachel lifted Ava's hands and kissed them. "How far gone are you, Momma?" she asked. Ava said nothing. Rachel lowered her hands. Was Ava's mind a blank slate now—a blackboard with no writing on it? Or were the doctors wrong? Did Ava understand everything she said but couldn't communicate with her? Was it a matter of return instead of intake?

People often referred to Alzheimer's sufferers as childlike. Was that true? Was her momma like a child? Or was she able to comprehend, but merely blocked by some internal barrier from responding to what she saw and heard?

The doctors said, "Doubtful." Still, Rachel wondered sometimes. But perhaps that would be worse for her momma—to be able to understand everything but respond to nothing. Like a prisoner behind a clear glass wall, able to see and hear what's happening on the outside but unable to communicate to those beyond the glass.

A jolt of thunder jarred Rachel from her musings. She glanced at her watch and felt the panic rise in her throat again. "I'm going to pack up your room," Rachel said. "We'll get things ready to take with you."

She stood and kissed her momma on the head. Then she moved to a stack of empty boxes Josey had placed in the corner, folding back the lid on the top one. Box in hand, she stepped to Ava's dresser and pulled out all the drawers. They contained all kinds of clothes—slacks, sweaters, socks, night-gowns, undergarments. With scurrying fingers, Rachel dropped the most worn items on the floor for later disposal, laid a few pieces on the bed for donation to the church Clothes Closet program, and threw the rest into the box. When the first box was full she loaded up a second one. Finished with the drawers, she grabbed another box and started cleaning off the top of the dresser, a mixed clutter of more family pictures, several perfume bottles, a couple of jewelry boxes, and a cigar box full of loose change.

Deliberately refusing to look at the pictures, she made short work of the odds and ends, dispatching the most recent of the photos to the box to go to the nursing home and the rest to a box that the movers would put into storage in her basement. Done with the dresser, she dusted off her hands and entered the bedroom closet. A row of shoes—still in their original boxes—sat neatly on the floor under the clothes.

Rachel knelt and counted the boxes—forty-eight of them. The shoes inside were half a size smaller than what she wore. "Feet like Tinkerbell," Ray used to say of Ava. "No bigger than a fairy's."

Rachel opened a shoebox and pulled out a pair of tan heels that Ava had bought almost ten years ago. She lifted out a shoe and held it for several seconds. Her momma, usually a most frugal woman, loved shoes and spent more money on them than on any other personal item.

"Shoes are what take you where you're going," Ava always said when somebody teased her about buying another pair. "So you best buy something that will take you there in style."

Rachel placed the shoe back in its box. A nursing home closet measured about four by four—nowhere near enough room for all these shoes. Her eyes teared at her next thought. Even if the closet was the size of a garage, Ava only wore bedroom slippers or tennis shoes these days. No need for anything else.

Rachel put the top on the shoebox. Maybe she could keep a few pair for herself, she decided, a few of the bigger ones. But she would give the rest to the church for dispersal to the less fortunate. Resigned, she grabbed another box and tossed one pair of black pumps, one pair of bedroom slippers, and one pair of tennis shoes into it. That's all Ava would need. The movers could handle the rest.

It took Rachel thirty more minutes to load up the rest of the belongings she planned to take to the nursing home. A couple of house robes, three dresses, a navy jacket, four warm up suits, all of them dark green. Her momma liked the loose-fitting jogging suits and wore one most of the time.

Looking around the closet, Rachel searched for anything else Ava just had to have. One of her Sunday hats? No, she didn't go to church anymore. A suitcase? Yes, a small one. Not that she took any trips, but she might need one when she went into the hospital. Those trips were more frequent these days. A rain coat? Okay, but not much else. Glancing around one more time, Rachel decided she had gathered everything her momma needed.

Strange, she thought leaving the closet, how much we can condense our belongings when circumstances force us to do it. Although surrounded by so much, we absolutely have to have only a very little: one or two changes of clothes, a pair of shoes, a comb or brush, a coat of some kind, a toothbrush, a few undergarments. When it all came right down to it, a person could make do on some mighty meager possessions . . . especially if the person's mind has moved out like a migrant worker leaving an old house.

Back in the bedroom, Rachel moved once more to Ava who had dozed off. Her chin rested on her chest at an odd angle. For a couple of seconds, Rachel stood still, her mind a jumble. How strange that this woman, so vibrant for most of her life, had become this empty shell. How was it the preacher put it once at a funeral when he wanted to make the point that the body of the deceased no longer contained the essence of the person? "The shell is here but the nut is gone." That's it, that's how the preacher said it.

Rachel grinned in spite of the situation. From what she heard later, the family of the deceased man hadn't taken too kindly to that statement. Seems they thought any reference to a nut had struck too close to home. Right now though, Rachel would have been glad to have a nutty Momma, or any other kind for that matter. She'd have preferred anything but the empty shell that sat so still in the rocker.

In the hallway the clock bonged again—it was 1:45. Rachel switched back into action. Only a couple more things to go through—a small highboy across from Ava's dresser, and the chest at the foot of the bed. The highboy took less than fifteen minutes, most of its contents left for the movers to load.

Rachel quickly pulled her chair to the chest and sat down by it. A "Hope Chest," that's what they called it in former years— a piece of furniture that held a young woman's belongings as she prepared for marriage. Rachel ran her fingers over the chest. Her momma had married a good man, an electrician named Ray Conner who spoke softly, smiled a lot, and treated everybody he met like a best friend. Although he had never become a wealthy man, he had put food on the table and a roof over their heads. Better still, he had provided steady love and simple wisdom.

Rachel glanced at the wall of pictures behind the bed. Ray smiled out from many of them—a moon-faced man with ears the size of small biscuits, and hair as dark as coal. In all the pictures he wore a wide toothy grin, like a boy with a funny secret he wanted to tell. Rachel's heart swelled. Though he had been her step-father, Ray had always treated her like his own biological child. She didn't know otherwise until she was 18.

Rachel unhooked the latch on the chest and flipped back the lid. The cedar wood smelled wonderful—fresh as a tree in the forest even after all these years.

Rachel picked quickly through the trunk, moved a stack of sweaters out, then several framed pictures. Under the pictures, she found a quilt—one she recognized from her childhood. It was decorated with swatches from some of the dresses she had outgrown. Ava always had a knack for such inventiveness—using what others might throw away to make beautiful things.

Her fingers playing on the quilt, Rachel glanced toward her momma. Ava still hadn't moved. Her head was still tilted to the side, her eyes closed, mouth slightly agape. Rachel wondered how she could sleep in such a position without hurting herself. A roll of thunder shook the house, and Rachel laid the quilt on the bed. Time was wasting. If she didn't go home at least for a few minutes before her appointment, Tim would feel hurt. Even as patient as he was, he still had his limits; and she didn't want to press them. The last thing she needed on Mother's Day was her sweet husband upset with her.

She pulled a man's old jacket from the chest and laid it on the floor. Next came a badly wrinkled, off-white linen dress, and a pair of matching gloves. A faded bathrobe with a frayed hem lay under the dress. Not recognizing any of the clothing, Rachel decided they could all go to the church. She looked to the bottom of the chest. A long black bag lay folded on the bottom. Rachel caught her breath. For several seconds, she stared at the bag. She knew what it contained.

Her eyes glanced several times back and forth between Ava and the bag. Then, not knowing anything else to do, she lifted out the bag and stretched it on the bed. She would take it home, she decided—put it in her closet for safekeeping. Who knew? Maybe Kara would wear it someday.

On her feet now, Rachel picked up three of the boxes she had packed for the nursing home and rushed them to her truck. The rain fell even harder now, and the wind had picked up. The top branches of the oak trees swayed overhead. Lightning cut the sky, followed closely by thunder. Black clouds rushed over in the rapid breeze.

Rachel shoved the boxes into the passenger seat of the truck and ran back to the house. In Ava's room again, she grabbed the black bag and started to leave. But then the lightning hit again and the lights flickered. The thunder boomed. Rachel told herself to slow down. She had to wait for Josey anyway. But where was she? Had the storm slowed her down?

Rachel laid the black bag back on the bed and decided to wait a few minutes before going back to the truck. She grabbed a towel from the bathroom and wiped her hair and face. Then she picked up the bag again and pulled up her chair by Ava. She touched her momma's hands. Ava jerked her eyes open and sat up straight. For an instant, Rachel thought she saw something behind the eyes, but the moment passed—the eyes were glazed over. Thunder shook the floors, and Ava twisted quickly and stared outside again.

Rachel patted her hand. "Not much of a Mother's Day, is it," she said softly.

Ava didn't respond.

"You were a good Momma," Rachel said, knowing it was true. Before she married Ray, Ava had cared for her all by herself. Then she mothered the three sons born to her and Ray. After his death, Ava provided for all of them. In Ava's arms, Rachel had never feared anything, at least not until the day she found out Ray wasn't her real daddy.

"I wish you had told me, though" she said, patting Ava's hand again, voicing the only thing she had ever held against her momma.

Ava didn't speak.

"It's the only thing you ever denied me," Rachel continued. "But it was a big one."

Ava stared out at the storm.

Rachel rearranged Ava's shawl. She was the mother now, she realized—mother to her momma. The daughter had become the parent, and it was a heavy load to bear.

"I've got our wedding dress," Rachel said. "Your momma wore it first, then you, then me."

Ava stared past the falling rain. Rachel thought of her appointment and hoped Josey would return soon. She ran her fingers over the garment bag's zipper. Her momma's wedding dress, her momma's before her, then hers. All three married in the same church, the Harmony United Methodist Church on

Main Street in downtown Rock Branch. Candles burning, good neighbors watching, a Methodist preacher doing the honors of leading each of the couples in their vows.

Rachel took the zipper and pulled it down. She lifted the dress out, dropped the bag to the floor, and laid the dress in her lap. It wasn't that fancy—just a simple, floor length white dress cut from a quality satin. Strapless, the dress had a matching jacket with satin buttons down the front. Cinched at the waist, the dress fluffed out over the hips and ran to the floor. A small, tasteful train trailed it at the heels. The tailored waist measured twenty inches and had never been altered.

Rachel wrapped her hands on either side of her waist and sucked in. Not twenty inches any more, but not yet twenty-five either. So far, her genes had taken good care of her. She thought of her daughter Kara—small, like all the women in her family. And the blonde hair took with blue eyes. Would she wear this dress the day she married? Would she have a twenty-inch waistline?

A jolt of lightning sizzled the sky, and Rachel glanced at her mother. Would Momma even be alive when Kara married? Probably not. Her doctor said she had another year or so at most. Rachel looked back at the dress and held it up to her cheek, rubbing the soft fabric against her skin. Tears rolled to the corners of her eyes as she let her worst fear escape.

With her body so much like her momma's, did everything else match too? Did her genes doom her to the same disease that had eaten away at Ava—a disease that entered a life like a ghost and never disappeared until it took you with it? Would she end up like Ava some day—sitting by a window with a blank stare on her face; unable to feed herself, clean herself, know her own name? The disease had attacked Ava so early in her life. Would that happen to her as well? Would she miss her granddaughter's wedding because she had no capacity to know it was happening? Maybe even worse, would Kara sit in a room somewhere years and years from now and clean out her belongings and prepare to put her in a nursing facility? Is that what she would want Kara to do? Or would she want her to find a way, no matter how tough on her family, to care for her in her own home?

Rachel rubbed away her tears with the hem of the dress. She was missing a lot of Kara's life—she knew that. She spent too much time at the real estate agency. That cost her other things too—hiking the mountain trails, taking picnics with Tim, and talking like they used to do.

Rachel laid the dress in her lap again. She had so little time for those kinds of things these days, so little time for quiet, for the nurture of her own soul. Most of the time she felt like a top spinning around and around, just a couple of spins away from banging into the wall or toppling over from too much speed. Though she loved Tim and knew he loved her, their relationship seemed frayed at the edges; and she never saw Kara until late in the day after picking her up from Mrs. Becker.

She wanted to change things but had no clue how. She was a doer like her momma, what could she say? She found meaning in what she accomplished—liked the notion of using her gifts to the fullest. Her work contributed to society. She helped people find places to live, houses they could make a home. It was noble toil. How could she give it up?

The phone in the entry hall rang, cutting off her thoughts. Laying the dress on the bed, Rachel rushed to the phone.

Maybe it was Josey, telling her she was on the way. Or maybe it was the retired couple; maybe the thunderstorms had caused them to change their minds about house hunting. For once, Rachel hoped that was true. On Mother's Day—at least this one—she wanted nothing more than to go home and spend the rest of the afternoon with her husband and daughter. ❧

∞∞∞

# CHAPTER THREE

# *Mysteries*

RACHEL PICKED UP THE PHONE AND HEARD TIM ON THE OTHER
end. "You finished yet?" he asked expectantly.

Rachel leaned on the table. "No, I'm waiting on Josey. She's
late coming back from the store."

"It's almost two. If you don't hurry, we won't see you all
afternoon."

Rachel heard the exasperation in his voice, an emotion he
hardly ever showed, but one she knew he had been feeling a
lot lately . . . with good reason.

"You know I have to do this," she said, trying to convince
herself as much as him. "We have to prepare for the movers
tomorrow."

Tim paused. Rachel could almost see him, his tall, lanky
body holding the phone like a baby holding a toy rattle. He
would not speak harshly to her, no matter how much she agi-
tated him. Normally, he had the disposition of a puppy—loyal,
happy, and pleased with simple things like food, shelter, and
somebody to rub him on the tummy every now and again.

"I'm not talking about your taking care of Mrs. Ava," he said.
"Take all the time you need for that. But I can't understand
this appointment. Can't you postpone it, at least for today?"

Rachel squeezed the phone. Though Tim seldom interfered

with her work, she felt resentful at his suggestion. It seemed invasive somehow, like he wanted to take control. "Real estate sales depend on the client," she said firmly. "When they want to see something, you show it to them."

Tim sighed. Rachel imagined him pushing his wavy brown hair off his forehead.

"Kara made you a Mother's Day card in Sunday school," he said. "She wants to give it to you."

Rachel's heart dropped. Feeling stressed, she had skipped church today—a rarity for her. "I'll come as soon as Josey gets back," she said. "Let Kara give me the card."

"I'd like to see you too," said Tim.

Rachel bit her lip. Tim was right. She should have refused the appointment—should have finished at Ava's, then hurried straight to her own family. But it was too late now. The retired couple wanted to see some expensive land a few miles out of Hendersonville, and she had no way to contact them and cancel the appointment.

"I'm about done with Momma," she said. "Just waiting on Josey."

"Just hurry," said Tim. "Kara wants to go down the street to play with a friend."

"Tell her she can go by four," said Rachel.

"Okay."

Rachel hung up and headed to the kitchen. A cup of tea, she decided—a cup of tea to calm down while she waited on Josey. Outside, a bolt of lightning split the sky and thunder followed, a shattering wave of sound that quivered the house. Wrapping her arms around her waist, Rachel suddenly felt chilled. Not a day for the weak of heart, she decided. Not a day for that at all.

Back in the master bedroom, Ava lifted her head at the clap of thunder. For a second she stared out the window as if expecting the glass to shatter. But then she placed her tiny feet on the floor and started to rock gently. The rain poured harder, a river pouring from the sky. Ava rocked a little faster as the rain gushed. Rock and rain, rock and rain. Another shot of lightning and thunder rolled over the house. Ava's feet pushed harder and harder on the floor. More rain fell. Her pace picked up so much the rocker tipped out and back, faster and faster, so that one would think she might flip it over backward or take off flying from the speed of it all.

But then, as if exhausted by its efforts, the rain suddenly stopped. Ava did too. Her feet braked on the hardwood floor, and she gazed out the window. Within seconds, the clouds started to break up. From somewhere deep in the storm, the sun forced its way through, and a ray of light bore its way to the ground. Within seconds, a rainbow formed in the west, and a shaft of light wider than a barn washed down and over Ava's house.

Ava's face caught the sun as it slipped in through her window, and she lifted a hand to shade her eyes. With a quick flutter of wings, a white dove landed on the windowsill and looked through the glass at her. The sun's rays enveloped Ava's head, illuminating it like a halo. She dropped her eyes and bent her chin against her chest to avoid the glare. But she couldn't. It lit up her head like a spotlight on a theater stage.

Everything in the room grew still. Ava lifted her chin and stared into the face of the dove. Her eyes, glassy and unfocused for close to a year, suddenly brightened. The eyes blinked, once, twice, three times. The dove cooed and fluttered its wings.

As if waking from a long sleep, Ava stretched her arms high over her head. After a couple of seconds, she slowly touched her toes to the floor and grabbed the chair's arms. The rocker eased forward as if hesitant to commit itself. Ava pushed gently out of it. Her shawl dropped to the floor. She seemed not to notice. The rocker tilted back, then forward, then settled into stillness. Ava took two small steps and reached the window. Her hands trembling, she leaned against the window frame and pushed up on it. It cracked but didn't budge. She bent at the waist and pushed up again. This time it scraped loose and slid up. A rush of air blew threw the screen, pushing Ava's hair back off her shoulders. The dove cooed. Ava smoothed down her hair. A touch of emotion played on her lips, not exactly a smile but a glimmer of something—joy maybe, or just sheer amazement. The dove cooed again, an insistent tone in its voice, and Ava nodded as if she understood its message. She twisted from the window and inspected her bedroom. Within seconds, her eyes fell on the wedding dress on the bed. She caught her breath and sagged back against the wall.

For a moment she stayed in place, her eyes fixed. Then, her steps as careful as a baby walking for the first time, she tottered to the bed and stood over the dress. Her forehead wrinkled as if trying to figure out a complex math problem. Then, though still unsteady, she bent and picked up the dress.

For a couple of seconds, her fingers gently rubbed the satin. A look of wonder crawled onto her face, the look of a blind woman suddenly able to see a waterfall once more. A tear rolled onto each cheek, and she touched the dress to the tears and soaked them into the garment just as her daughter had done only a few minutes ago. As if handling something sacred, she carefully lowered the dress back on the bed and sat down beside it. Her eyes landed on the pile of clothes that Rachel had stacked on the floor. For a second, she studied them. Then she moved off the bed, grabbed up the clothes and sorted through them. When she reached the linen dress, she laid it beside the wedding dress, then dropped the rest of the clothes back to the floor. With one of the dresses in each hand, she moved back to the window.

At the window, she pushed both dresses together and held them steadily for several seconds. The sun landed on the dresses, and they warmed in her hands. The wedding dress seemed to glow in the sunshine, its whiteness now almost too brilliant to look at. The dove fluttered its wings as if applauding Ava's accomplishment.

Satisfied with the response, Ava laid the wedding dress on the back of the rocker and held the wrinkled one up to her body like a young woman in a dress shop measuring it for a fit. Apparently pleased with what she saw, she slipped off her robe, dropped it to the floor, and carefully pulled the linen dress over her head. It slipped on easily. Smoothing down the wrinkles, Ava eased back to the rocker, picked up the wedding dress and sat down. A small smile played on her lips, and she turned back toward the sun, her eyes clear. In contrast to the smile, a new pair of tears slid down her face. She ran her hands over the wedding dress again and again and rocked out and back, out and back, out and back . . .

∞∞∞

Back in the kitchen, Rachel sat at the dining table, sipped from her tea and tried to relax. Though he had said little, she knew Tim was frustrated with her. He took days like this seriously—Valentine's Day, Mother's and Father's days, birthdays. He insisted that they do family things on them.

"You never know when your last chance will come," he always said. "Better spend time with each other while you can."

Though Rachel agreed with the sentiment, she didn't always stick to the plan as closely as he did. She felt guilty about it but, hey, she had things to do and holidays rolled around too often.

She poured another cup of tea and stared out the window at the rainbow left by the storm. A sign of God's favor, she remembered, after forty days and nights of rain. She sipped her tea and wondered why God had never given her a sign.

She dropped a lump of sugar into her tea and put aside her musings about the rainbow. She had to finish the packing, no time for rainbows. She hung her head. Putting her momma in a nursing home made her feel ashamed. No self-respecting mountain family turned their kin out like that. She didn't deserve any sign from God. No matter that she had no option regarding Ava.

She couldn't quit her job. It meant too much to her. Yeah, she needed to slow down some, find some balance, some time for Tim and Kara. But every time she tried to cut down her hours, she ended up miserable. Her career made her feel valuable, like she had accomplished something, made something of herself. But was that as crucial as she made it? Was making a contribution to the business world as important as spending more hours with her husband and daughter?

Unable to settle her dilemma, Rachel stood, poured the rest of her tea down the sink and headed back to her momma's room. Though she knew her life was out of whack in some crucial areas, she had no clue how to fix it. No matter how you sliced the pie, she felt driven to make something of herself, and she couldn't do that staying home all day.

⋄⋄⋘⋙⋄

Even before she saw Ava in her rocker, Rachel sensed something different in the bedroom air. Maybe it was the breeze that stirred the bangs on her forehead as she opened the door. Or maybe it was the open window she saw the instant she walked in. But by the time her eyes landed on Ava, Rachel knew something major had changed. Then she saw the wedding dress in Ava's lap, the wrinkled one on her body. What in the world?

Rachel reached Ava in a second and started to speak, but found she couldn't. She lifted an arm, but her momma turned to her before she could point, and Rachel saw something in her eyes that made her heart stop. Rachel's hand dropped lifelessly to her side.

"Sit . . . sit down," whispered Ava, her voice scratchy. "We need . . . need to . . . talk."

Rachel stood with mouth agape, too shocked to move.

"Sit," Ava rasped again, a bony finger pointing to a chair.

Rachel jumped as if electrocuted. "Momma!" she exclaimed, finally finding her voice. "I don't understand . . . what . . . what . . .?"

"Sit . . ." Ava said a third time. "I don't know how long . . . how long I can . . ." She pointed to the chair, her finger shaking.

"I'll call a doctor!" Rachel said, her eyes frantic.

Ava shook her head. "No . . . no time." she said. "I need . . . need to say . . . say . . ." She grabbed Rachel's arm and squeezed hard. "Listen . . ." she insisted. "No time for a doctor."

Rachel bit her lip. Though she didn't understand what was happening, she sensed her momma was right. Time was short. Whatever had caused this probably wouldn't last long. She pulled up the chair by Ava and took her momma's hands.

"Remember the night . . . night . . . you turned eighteen?" asked Ava.

Rachel's arms felt like lead pipes. Her face tingled. How could she forget the night Ray died and she learned he wasn't really her father? She went from grief to shock, to confusion, to fury all in one evening. Sadness and anger are a devastating combination.

"I never . . . told you who your . . . your real daddy was," said Ava.

Rachel tried to swallow, but her throat felt as if it had a lump the size of an apple in it.

"I couldn't tell you then," said Ava. "But I need to tell you now. For your . . . your sake and his."

Rachel's heart thudded. "I don't know, Momma," she said. "What difference does it make now? Let me call a doctor. They can—"

Ava pulled her hands away, rubbed the wedding dress, and peered past the window, ignoring Rachel. The dove remained on the sill, its feathers bright. "You gonna' let me say what I need to say or not?" asked Ava.

"But why now?"

Ava shook her head. "I don't exactly know. But I've got to tell you. That's why I've . . . I've come back."

Rachel knew she couldn't argue anymore. She wanted to know what Ava had to say, wanted it more than anything in her whole life. "Okay, Momma," she said. "I'm listening."

Facing her again, Ava patted her hand. "Okay," she said. "Here it is . . . Your father's name is . . . is David Thorton."

Rachel stiffened at the name, though she had never heard it before. Her fingers throttled the chair's arms. She heard her own teeth grind. She repeated the name. "David Thorton."

Ava nodded. "He lives on the other side of Hendersonville."

Anger curled up like a snake in Rachel's stomach. Whoever this man was, he lived close by.

"Does he know about me?" she asked.

"Yes, for a long time."

Rachel chewed her lower lip. David Thorton knew about her but had never cared enough to meet her, had never given any indication of knowing she existed. Her anger burned higher, a fire with gas thrown on it. Rachel started to speak, but Ava cut her off.

"Don't say anything," Ava said. "He's a good man, a church-going man. And he loves you; I want you to know that."

"I don't think so," argued Rachel, unable to hide her feelings. "Least not that I've ever seen."

"You don't know everything," said Ava.

Rachel considered the matter and told herself to hear Ava out. But something inside fought against listening. Thorton didn't care about her. Why should she care about him? Her resentment grew with each second that passed.

"I know all I want to know," she said, her feelings hurt so badly she didn't stop to consider what she was doing, what she was saying. "Enough that I don't want you to make excuses for this David Thorton, whoever he is."

Ava's mouth wrinkled with disapproval. "You need to understand," she whispered.

Rachel tried to stop, to give Ava a chance to explain. But a gush of unpleasant memories flooded through her head, memories that the name "David Thorton" unleashed again, washing out any notion of graciousness toward him. "I understand plenty," she said. "I find out at eighteen that Ray isn't really my dad, but you can't tell me who is. I beg you for months, but you're busy grieving over Ray's death, and I know I shouldn't ask anymore. Then I go off to college and try to forget about it, get on with my life. I do that, make something of myself, not letting the fact that I'm a bastard child stop me. But today I show up to move you to a nursing home and you . . . you . . . I don't know how, but you can suddenly talk again. And you're telling me that a man who lives less than an hour's drive away is my father. But he's never shown one bit of interest in me. Is that about it . . . what I ought to understand?"

"There's more to the story," Ava sighed. "A . . . a lot more." She hung her head as if it were suddenly very heavy.

"There always is," Rachel snarled.

"I was only a girl," said Ava, brushing a wisp of hair from her face. "But I loved . . . loved your father, you have to believe that." Her voice slowed and her shoulders sagged. She looked like a battery starting to run low. Her next words barely crawled from her lips. "He loved me too."

Rachel found it hard to breathe. She sensed her momma

wouldn't have enough energy to say much more. At least not for awhile.

"You were born . . . born in Missouri, near St. Louis," Ava whispered. "I lived with your Aunt Wilma. My father sent me there."

Panicked by her momma's weakness, Rachel almost yelled her next question. "Why didn't you and this David Thorton marry? If you were so much in love?"

Ava rubbed the wedding dress like a child rubbing a security blanket. Rachel stared at the dress, and then back at her momma.

"I wanted . . . wanted to wear this," whispered Ava, looking intently at it in her lap.

"You did wear it," said Rachel, but she wasn't sure she understood. "When you married Ray."

Ava smiled, but it seemed to take a toll on her. "Ray was a good man," she whispered.

"He was," agreed Rachel. "But you and Thorton, why didn't you marry?"

Ava lifted the wedding dress to her face, rubbing it gently on her cheek. "Oh how I wanted to wear this," she repeated.

Rachel started to ask again why she and Thorton hadn't married. But Ava looked spent. Perspiration had broken out on her forehead, and her breath seeped in and out in shallow pulls and pushes.

The telephone in the entry hall rang. Rachel wondered if it was Josey, or maybe Tim again. For a second, she waited on Ava to continue, but she didn't. The phone rang again.

"Get the . . . the phone," whispered Ava. "Maybe it's . . . Tim."

Grateful that Ava had remembered Tim's name, Rachel

weighed the situation. Should she leave Ava or ignore the call? But Tim was already mad. And maybe a minute or two to rest would give Ava some time to regroup a little, gain enough strength to tell more of the story.

On her feet, Rachel decided to answer the phone. She would tell the caller she would call right back, then rush back to Ava. She hurried across the room. At the door, a sudden chill hit her and she shivered. Worried that Ava would get cold, she pivoted back to put the shawl over her momma's shoulders. She instantly saw the change and rushed back to the rocker. Her heart racing, she squatted in front of Ava. "Momma!" she called. "I'm here, Momma! Don't leave me again. Not yet. Momma! Momma!"

Though she called out again and again, Rachel knew the truth. The vacant stare had returned to Ava's face. The dove had disappeared from the windowsill. A new blanket of black clouds covered the sky.

Sensing something she didn't want to name, Rachel started to cry. As if trying to coax life back into a dead person, she rubbed Ava's hands and arms, stood and stroked her hair and hugged her neck. "Come back, Momma," she begged. "I'm sorry I didn't listen to you, let you finish what you had to say."

Ava didn't respond. Her eyes gazed out the window as she continued to rub the wedding dress.

Back on her knees, Rachel squinted into Ava's eyes and hoped to find some light in them once again. Guilt hit her with a crushing blow that almost made her bend at the waist in pain.

"I'm sorry, Momma," she sobbed again. "So sorry . . ." For several minutes the sobs wracked her body. She had wasted this chance, talked when she should have listened, let her anger use up too much time, kept Ava from telling everything she had come to tell. As usual, she had pushed too hard, and by doing so had let a golden opportunity slip through her fingers, truth escaping her grasp like air. Now she could do nothing about it.

After another minute of sobbing, Rachel's tears ran dry, and she gathered her emotions together and folded them away. Okay, she figured, she had made a mistake. It wasn't the first one and it wouldn't be the last. Do the best you can, she told herself. Take a lemon and make lemonade. That motto had held her in good stead a long time. No reason to drop it now. Don't let circumstances wreck you. Deal with them, no matter how tough, no matter how painful.

Finished with her inner pep talk, Rachel rose and turned to the window. Like Ava, she looked out at the storm that had regrouped and was once more pouring water and lightning out of the sky. Her hand on Ava's shoulder, Rachel took a deep breath. Though she had not learned everything, she had learned the name of her father. In a way mysterious, maybe even miraculous, the wedding dress had brought Ava back long enough for her to tell Rachel part of a story that would surely change her life forever. Whether for the better or worse, she had no way of knowing.

Slowly, gently, Rachel lifted the wedding dress from her momma's lap and laid it back on the bed. Then she laid the shawl back over Ava's shoulders and gave her one more hug. Somehow she knew the truth. Her momma would never speak again. She kissed her on the forehead. Now she had to decide what to do with what Ava had told her. ❧

*We don't know each other's secrets*

*quite so well as we flatter ourselves*

*we do. We don't always know our*

*own secrets as well as we might.*

OLIVER WENDELL HOLMES

※※※※

# CHAPTER FOUR

# *Confusions*

IN THE WEEK AFTER MOTHER'S DAY, RACHEL WALKED AROUND AS if someone had smacked her in the head with a washtub—knocked off balance but not enough to put her into total unconsciousness. As planned, she and her stepbrothers put Ava in Mixon's Nursing Home on Monday morning. The transfer went off without a hitch—papers signed, belongings loaded into the assigned room, tearful goodbyes as they left her behind. Though she watched closely all morning, Rachel saw no sign of any further awareness in Ava. Whatever had happened to her on Sunday had not reoccurred overnight. Though not expecting anything else, the realization saddened Rachel. She still had so much she didn't know, so much she needed to ask.

After leaving the nursing home, Rachel headed straight back to work. No matter what Ava had told her, she had a schedule to keep. For the rest of the week, she kept regular hours at the office—about ten a day—then rushed home to help Tim with supper. After supper, she spent some time with Kara, then put her to bed and collapsed onto the sofa. Because she didn't know what she was going to do with the secret Ava had revealed, she didn't tell Tim or anybody else about Ava's mysterious re-emergence from the fog of Alzheimer's. Why should she? Tim would have a million questions she couldn't answer, and he'd want to know what Ava had said, and she didn't want to tell him. At least not yet. Why reveal something that everyone involved had kept secret for so long—something that might do more harm than good if it became general knowledge? Until she decided how to handle all this, she would just keep it a secret.

In an effort to stop wondering about David Thorton—the kind of man he was, what he looked like, what he did—she bought and read three books about Alzheimer's. A doctor had explained everything back when Ava first started showing symptoms, and Rachel had forgotten little of it, she still wanted to refresh her knowledge. The books didn't contradict what she already knew. But they did reenforce a few things, like the fact that the older people become the more likely they are to experience some degree of the disease. Only three to five percent of people under sixty-five have the affliction, but forty percent over eighty have it. And a specific gene called ApoE/4 means you have a greater chance of suffering from the disease than if you don't have it. And, worst of all, people with a first-degree relative—sibling or parent—tend to have the illness with greater frequency than the rest of the population.

Knowing all this didn't make Rachel feel any better. But it did remind her that Ava had no control over anything that happened. For that matter, no one else did either. Alzheimer's is a thief that steals the mind, and nobody has a security system to keep it from intruding.

Though resigned to that fact, Rachel did call a specialist in Asheville on Tuesday. She asked him if people ever come out of their Alzheimer's coma—ever make sudden, dramatic shifts back to consciousness. To her surprise, he told her "yes."

"It's been reported on rare occasions," the doctor said. "A person will have a flash of lucidity, a quick burst when he or she can talk again and recognize people."

"But how?" asked Rachel. "Nothing I've read mentions this."

"Nobody knows for sure how," said the doctor. "But one theory suggests that a person might have a small stroke; that stroke somehow breaks through the clogged up parts of the brain. Sort of like a bolt of lightning burning away a thicket of brush. You can't predict it, and it doesn't last long, but it has been known to happen."

"But why doesn't anybody write about this?" she asked.

"Easy. It happens so rarely. Why tell people something that almost never happens? Why get their hopes up when there really is no reason for hope?"

After thanking the doctor, Rachel hung up and called Ava's local doctor. She figured he needed to check her for any permanent changes, any sign of a stroke. But he was out of town for two weeks. She made an appointment for Ava to see him three days after he returned.

Having read the books and checked into the medical situation, Rachel ran out of diversions, and Thorton's name started popping up in her head more and more often.

"But it doesn't matter any more," she argued to herself. "The man has demonstrated that he wants nothing to do with you."

She could understand it while Ray was living. Thorton didn't want to upset a happy family. But later, after Ray died? Thorton could have made contact then.

Rachel knew, of course, that Thorton surely had all kinds of excuses not to introduce himself. No doubt they were legitimate ones, too. Perhaps he had a family of his own, probably did. A secret daughter would surely upset that. Ava had said he was a church-going man. Nothing like an illegitimate kid to poke a hole in a good Christian reputation. Yeah, Thorton had good reasons to stay away from her. She could understand his predicament. Why bother him now? Ruin his life? Or at least complicate it a good bit.

For that matter, why bother herself? She had done just fine without David Thorton. She could keep on doing just fine. To confront him seemed like a sign of weakness, like a helpless woman who needed a father figure in her life to survive. Well, she had made her way pretty well with Ray as her daddy and didn't need a new man in that role. Bury it all, she argued— like garbage in a landfill.

But she found that tough to do. No matter what she did or where she went, Rachel continued the internal debate. Ava's revelation meant nothing. It was a noble but misguided effort to clear up the one and only thing that had remained unsaid between mother and daughter as the Alzheimer's worsened; a valiant effort to soothe some unspoken guilt chewing away at Ava's deep subconscious. But the name meant nothing to Rachel. Why should she care about David Thorton? So what if he and her momma had once shared the ultimate intimacy? So what if his genetic code pumped through her body, a current of life intermingling with the one Ava had given her? So what if she had often stood in front of the mirror as a child and wondered why she looked so little like Ray—or Ava either for that matter, except for their size? So what if she now knew the name of somebody she might look like? David Thorton meant no more to her than a stray dog would mean to one of the puppies that it sired on a spring-night spree.

Repeating that over and over, Rachel spent the week making sure she stayed busy. Her free time was consumed just visiting Ava every day—sometimes twice, early morning and late at night—sitting by her for at least an hour each time, and longer when she could. Every now and then Ava's eyes flickered for a second, and Rachel thought she saw a glimmer of awareness in them. But the flicker always disappeared as quickly as it came, and Rachel figured she had just imagined it.

When not with Ava or at work, Rachel filled up her hours at home: meals to cook; clothes to wash, dry, iron, and fold; floors to vacuum and sweep; toilets to scrub; beds to make; dishes to clean. At night she fell into bed in a state of total exhaustion—her body feeling like dead weight, her mind numbed by constant activity.

On a deep level, Rachel knew what she was doing. By elevating her already-intense activity level to an even higher pitch, she used up most of her time and energy and left nothing over to do much thinking. That's what she figured she most needed—one dose of hurry after another, a list of things to do that covered the front of the refrigerator like a blanket on a bed. Drive here, sign this, volunteer for that, if you want something done, ask a busy person to do it and Rachel was the busiest person anyone knew, and she never said "no."

In spite of frenzied efforts, though, she couldn't turn off her questions. The nights were the worst, after Tim had fallen asleep. She lay beside him, listened to his breathing and wondered if Thorton was a good man like Tim? Or was he a jerk, as she suspected—a selfish lout who used people for his own pleasure and then cast them aside?

For hour after hour she lay in bed and stared at the ceiling, the dark room a black canvas on which her mind drew all kinds of pictures—pictures she closed her eyes and clenched the sheets against seeing; pictures of David Thorton.

Try as she might, she found it impossible to forget him. Did he have a tiny cleft in his chin like she did? or a birthmark in the shape of Oklahoma on the back of his right thigh? or a second toe that tended to bend outward as if trying to run from the big one. Though hating herself for it, Rachel kept imagining the face of the man who had fathered her, wondering what kind of eyes he had, what body type, whether his hair had turned gray like Ava's, what he did for a living. In a town as small as Hendersonville, he probably knew a lot of people and had a lot of friends. Was he a happy man, pleased with his accomplishments? Or was he haunted and sad, bothered by the fact that he had a child he had never claimed?

She thought about what he might do if she suddenly showed up on his doorstep? Would he welcome her, wrap his arms around her and tell her he had wanted this moment to come for a long time? Or would he slam the door in her face and deny her? Would he protect his reputation?

Every night that week she squeezed her eyes tighter and tighter and told herself to sleep. But little sleep came. By the time the next Sunday rolled around Rachel's appearance had suffered greatly. Her eyes sank darkly into her skull, her hair hung lifeless on her shoulders, and her lips were so thin it seemed like someone had taken the sides of her face and pulled them back toward her ears.

Rising out of bed that morning, Rachel looked in the mirror and knew she had to do something. Regardless of the consequences, she couldn't go on like this. It wasn't fair to Kara and Tim. Her jaw set, she made a decision.

The morning passed slowly, but she managed to endure it. She attended church with Tim and Kara; then she fixed, ate, and cleaned up Sunday dinner with them. About two hours later, after Tim had fallen asleep watching a golf tournament on T.V., Rachel dropped Kara at a friend's house and climbed into her truck. Starting the engine, she debated the matter one last time—go to Thorton or not? She thought of Ava, the miracle of her sudden ability to talk, the fact that she said she had come back to tell her the name of her father. Ava wanted her to know this. But why? Rachel could imagine only one reason. Ava wanted her to meet Thorton. Ava had come back precisely so she could have this opportunity.

Sure of her decision, Rachel left her house and drove twenty-six-and-three-tenths miles to a cluster of small stores outside of Hendersonville. She parked the truck and hustled into a local restaurant with the name "Ernestine's Eatery," written in bold red paint across the door. She settled into a booth and ordered pie and coffee. When the waitress brought the pie, Rachel asked if she had a phone book she could borrow. A few seconds later the waitress returned and handed her the book.

Her fingers shaky, Rachel flipped through the pages. In small towns like Hendersonville, few people had unlisted numbers. Surely, she would find Thorton's number. Her eyes landed on David and Louise Thorton, 5452 Meadow Lane Road, 704-885-1134. Just like that, a name and a number. David Thorton did exist. What had seemed so unreal now took on a life: a living, breathing human being that lived in a house and had a phone number listed in a book.

Rachel tried to catch her breath. So what if she had actually pinpointed Thorton's location? Leave it alone for his sake and hers. She took a bite of the pie. Though debating what to do next, she pulled a pen from her purse and wrote Thorton's address and phone number on a napkin and laid it on the table. Another bite of pie followed as she considered her next move.

"Who you looking for?"

Rachel closed the phone book and glanced up at the waitress who had suddenly appeared.

"Oh, nobody," she said, though much too quickly.

"I know most everybody in town," said the waitress. "You give me a name, I bet I can tell you where they live; not the phone number though—don't know all of them."

"I expect not," Rachel mumbled, wishing the waitress would go away. "Too many numbers for anybody to know."

The waitress poured Rachel a re-fill of coffee, then nodded at the napkin on the table. "You looking for Meadow Lane?" she asked, noting the address Rachel had written on the napkin.

Rachel started to deny it but then knew that made no sense. What difference did it make if a waitress at Ernestine's Eatery knew she wanted a phone number of somebody living on Meadow Lane? "Yeah," she said, sipping her coffee. "You know where that is?"

"You bet," said the waitress. "About two miles. Go up a half mile, turn left at the red barn. Go another mile, turn right at the first road past the bridge. That's Meadow Lane. A real pretty road, some nice houses out there. Looking for anybody in particular?"

Rachel sat the coffee cup down. She would say nothing else

to this nosy waitress. "Can I get my check?" she asked.

The waitress pursed her lips, almost as if in disapproval. "No problem."

A minute or so later, she returned, bill in hand. Rachel handed her a five-dollar bill. The waitress pulled change from the front of her apron. "Meadow Lane is a pretty road," she said. "A banker lives out there, the high school football coach, several of the important folks."

"Thanks," said Rachel, standing. "You've been a big help."

"No problem," said the waitress. "You come back to see us, now."

Nodding, Rachel left the restaurant. In her truck, she sat for several minutes and once more tried to figure what to do. Go home and forget all this? Or go to David Thorton's house?

But what would she do there? She had no idea. She laid her head on the steering wheel. Her body ached for sleep. She thought of her momma, of the unexpected conversation of last week. Ava had said she had come back to tell her the name of her father. Was that for Ava's benefit? Had guilt been eating away at her, like a sharp stone turning in her heart, cutting into her with its rough edges? Had Ava come to help herself? Or had she spoken the name for her daughter's sake, shared the long-hidden identity of David Thorton because she knew that Rachel needed to close the circle of her own identity?

Her head throbbing, Rachel realized she had no way to answer her questions unless she at least saw David Thorton. Maybe she wouldn't need to meet him. But she had to see what he looked like. Perhaps that would do it. Just get a glimpse, then leave him alone.

Starting the truck, she pushed her bangs from her face and

pulled onto the highway. Though not familiar with Meadow Lane, she had traveled this area some with her work, and it took her less than ten minutes to find the road she wanted. Steering carefully, she eased toward 5452. There! On the mailbox!

Driving past the house, she turned around about a quarter of a mile away and cruised back. The waitress had been right about the houses. Thorton's was a two-story white brick colonial with four columns, a set of large double doors, and a three-car garage. A well-manicured lawn at least three hundred feet wide and equally as deep fronted it. A variety of oaks, maples, and pines gave character to the lawn; and someone had planted a variety of flowers around the sidewalk, which snaked from the driveway to the front door.

Rachel pulled to the curb, threw the truck into park, and switched off the engine. Her fingers turning white as she squeezed the wheel, she faced her father's house. Though hating herself for the weakness that brought her there, Rachel realized she had to face this. Kind of like a phobia—to overcome the fear you have to endure the worst of it, show yourself you can fight it hand to hand and come out the victor.

A warm sun heated the truck's windshield. Rachel rolled down the window. In the distance she heard a lawn mower running. A tiny breeze drifted over her face. From all outward appearances, Thorton lived a pleasant life. A house this size meant he surely had a family, a good career too. Thorton was a man of stature. A model citizen no doubt—a model citizen who had fathered a child out of wedlock but never taken responsibility for his actions.

Rachel's lip curled in scorn. How dare David Thorton do so

well—receive such respect. How long would the folks of Hendersonville respect him if they knew what she knew?

A car drove past, breaking Rachel's thoughts. She started to drive away but then heard a door open. She glanced back at Thorton's house. A teenage boy hustled out the door, jumped into a car, backed out, and sped away. Watching his car disappear around a curve, Rachel remembered her own teenage years—one day in particular: her birthday, when she learned Ray wasn't her real father, when he died from a car accident . . .

Ava had called her at school. A logging truck traveling too fast around a curve on a rainy day had fishtailed on a mountain road about four miles from their house. The truck plowed into Ray's car, pinning it and him against the side of Smoker's Ridge. An ambulance rushed Ray to the hospital where one doctor set his broken legs and another operated on his lacerated face and skull. He had a serious concussion. His brain started to swell. The doctors threw their whole arsenal at his injuries, but nothing helped. By the next morning his face had swollen so tight he couldn't open his eyes.

Ava stayed by him all night while Rachel took care of the boys at home. The next morning though, she dropped the boys off at school and sped to the hospital. She found Ava by Ray's side, her hands stroking his forehead with a wet cloth. Rachel pulled up a chair by the bed and the three of them stayed that way the rest of the morning. Just before lunch, Ava took a break to visit the bathroom. Rachel moved to Ray, her hands touching his. His fingers were hot. Ray's eyes cracked opened as he felt her touch.

"You ought . . .ought to be in school," he said, his words

slurred by the medication the doctors had given him.

Rachel shook her head. "I'm where I need to be," she said.

Ray closed his eyes. A monitor beeped. Rachel looked up at the drip, drip, drip of the i.v. bag hanging by the bed. Ray gripped her hands.

"I tried . . . tried to do right by . . . by you," he said.

"You're a great dad," she said, her eyes tearing at the realization that Ray was trying to say goodbye, trying to make sure he had cleared up any last minute business just in case he never again had the chance.

"I treated you like my . . . my own daughter," he said, a single tear sliding from each eye and rolling back to his pillow. "Loved you like—"

Rachel held her breath. What was Ray saying? She heard her momma step up from behind. Ray stopped as Ava moved back to him. Rachel turned to Ava, a question on her face, then back to Ray. But she didn't know how to ask him what he meant, since he had so little strength left and she didn't want him wasting it. Though confused, she eased back into her chair.

For the rest of the day she and Ava watched over Ray, never leaving his side even for a moment. That night, just past dark, Rachel left for home to make dinner for the boys. Her momma called two hours later. Ray had died, breathing his last at just past 8:30. Rachel put away the birthday cake Ava had baked. They never ate it.

They buried Ray three days later—Ava, Rachel, and the boys throwing dirt on his coffin in the Hillside Cemetery about a mile out of Rock Branch. It took Rachel another two weeks to find the courage to ask her momma about Ray's last words to her, the words about treating her like his own daughter.

At first Ava tried to deflect the issue. "He was under medication," she said. "Out of his head."

Rachel insisted that wasn't true. Ray knew what he was saying. Finally, her shoulders slumped, Ava fell into a chair and told her the truth. Ray was not her biological father. No, she would not identify the man who was, not now at least. Someday, when Rachel was older, when she could understand more, she would tell her everything. But not now. She didn't have the strength to deal with it, Ava said, not so soon after Ray's death. Later, when her spirits re-grouped some, perhaps then she could handle the emotions it would stir up in her.

Too confused to argue, Rachel let it drop for a long time. Late that summer though, as she made plans to leave for college, she approached Ava one more time with the subject. But Ava, still struggling with her grief, refused to say anything more. "It won't do anybody any good to go digging up past dirt," she insisted. "Not you, not him, and not me. Not now anyway. So, please, I'm begging you, leave it alone."

Not knowing what else to do, Rachel let it rest. Ava had too many problems for her to push any harder. So what if she was an illegitimate child? It hadn't stopped her to this point.

Repeating often that her parentage didn't matter, Rachel moved to Raleigh to go to college. She tried to leave the past behind, reminding herself that Ava would never have engaged in pre-marital relations with a man unless she loved him dearly, loved him with a love beyond measure, a love greater than any she could imagine. Such a love had to be a noble thing, she concluded, not something to cause her any shame.

Unfortunately, however, Rachel felt shame every day, a

shame so deep she wondered if people might see it on her face, like a livid red scar burned into her flesh.

And Ava had lied to her about everything! What a hypocrite! She claimed to follow the Lord, but she had gotten pregnant without a husband and brought disgrace to everybody in her family.

Fueled by her anger, Rachel poured herself into her studies and vowed that she would rise above her embarrassing history. In three and a half years, she earned her business degree with highest honors. She spent a year in Raleigh on a management track in a bank. She met Tim at a church single's retreat. His family lived about thirty miles from hers, over in Stillwater. After nine months of courtship, he asked her to marry him, and she readily accepted.

Within a year of their honeymoon, they decided they both loved the mountains and wanted to move back there. They chose Rock Branch because Ava gave them ten acres of land not far from her place, and they built a small house on it. Tim drove out and back to Stillwater to manage his dad's heating and air conditioning business, and Rachel hooked up with Blue Ridge Real Estate located in Hendersonville. It didn't take her long to make her mark. A woman with something to prove, she started as an agent, moved up to manager within two years, took half ownership of the place within ten. "Rush It Rachel," that's who she was, a woman bound to make a lot of money, a woman determined to show people she had sub-stance, value, somebody who . . .

Rachel heard a door open again and she blinked back to the present, to David Thorton's house. A stocky man walked out the front door, his navy suit neatly pressed, his white shirt and striped tie the picture of small town, upper class style. She knew instantly the man was Thorton. He had a cleft in his chin like hers and a round forehead too. Even from this distance, she recognized herself in his stride, the way he tilted slightly to the left as he walked.

The resemblance didn't soothe her nerves any. It angered her instead, made her feel even more that Thorton was a selfish man, so selfish he never claimed his daughter.

He's headed to church, Rachel figured. Going to show off as a man of the Lord. Rachel felt hatred boil up in her chest, a feeling she had never really experienced. It tasted like rust and sour milk, a mixture she couldn't imagine drinking. But there it was, as real as anything she had ever known. Ready to confront Thorton with his sins, she reached for the door handle. Let him lie his way through this, she thought, let him tell me I'm crazy, dare me to prove what I'm saying.

The door to the house opened again and a woman who had to be Louise Thorton stepped out. Rachel let go the door handle. The woman looked pleasant, not mean at all. About the same height and build as Ava, she had her hair, dark but streaked with gray, pinned up and off her face. She wore a tan suit, not too fancy, but trim and tailored.

Rachel took a quick breath. Maybe Mrs. Thorton sang in the church choir, served in the clothes closet, taught kids in Sunday school. If so, she wasn't the kind of woman who deserved to hear what Rachel wanted to say.

While hesitating, another notion came to Rachel. How would she prove what Ava had said? By matching blood types? But that was complicated. And why would David Thorton agree to such a thing? And if he wouldn't do it voluntarily, could she make him do it—force him to go to court and prove he wasn't her father? Would a court take her word that he was? Probably not.

Rachel watched Louise and David Thorton climb into a black sedan, back out of the driveway, and head down the road. Unsure what else to do, she followed them a second later, her car lights blinking on as the sun started to drop. ❀

∞∞∞

# CHAPTER FIVE

# *Decisions, Again*

THE WEATHER BROKE OFF HOTTER THAN NORMAL THE NEXT WEEK —a quick shift to humid summer at least a month earlier than normal. Keeping her air conditioner on high, Rachel drove her clients around the mountains of Rock Branch, pointing them to this piece of land here and that cozy chalet there. Refusing to be distracted by her own problems, she once more threw herself into the job—her focus even more intense than last week, words quicker, steps more rapid as she moved in and out of the car to show people the property she hoped to sell them.

By the end of the week, she had closed three sales—a total value of almost five hundred thousand dollars. At an average of four percent per sale, her commission added up to about twenty thousand bucks. A good week in anybody's book, even "Rush It Rachel's." At the office, everyone congratulated her and told her she should take a break and let somebody else have a chance to make some money.

Pretending pleasure at her exploits, Rachel smiled widely and graciously accepted the kidding. Inside though, she felt as empty as a beggar who hadn't eaten for a week—which, for the most part, she hadn't. Whereas in the previous week she couldn't sleep much, now she couldn't eat too well either. With her mind on Thorton almost every waking minute, her stomach drew up like a closed sack that somebody had stapled together at the top. By the end of the week, she had lost at least five pounds—a lot for a woman who barely weighed a hundred at the beginning.

In between her business appointments, she made two other quick trips to Hendersonville to do some quiet checking on Thorton. What she found didn't surprise her. Thorton was the principal of Hendersonville High School, the chairman of the town's largest men's club, and a former mayor. He had two grown children, a son and a daughter, and three grandchildren. The boy that Rachel had seen leaving his house was a grandson. As she had figured, Thorton was a highly respected man.

For the one-hundredth time she wondered if maybe Ava had made a mistake by giving her Thorton's name. What good did it do her to know, if she couldn't confront him? But if she confronted him, what did that mean for his life and hers? She felt like someone had given her a great gift but then told her she couldn't open it.

On the last trip she made to Hendersonville that week, she drove back to Ernestine's Eatery, pulled Thorton's number from her purse, dropped some change in a phone outside and dialed. Four rings later, a woman answered. Rachel hung up. Back in the truck, she wondered what she would have done if Thorton had picked up. Would she have talked to him? told him her name? spilled out the whole situation? She didn't know.

Friday finally arrived. Rachel remained confused about what she wanted to do next. Leaving the office after a hectic day, she drove home, threw herself into a chair in the den, and closed her eyes, her body worn out. Already home, Tim eased over, gave her a kiss and stroked her hair. Though regretting it instantly, Rachel brushed his hand away. Tim stepped back a pace.

"What's wrong?" he asked.

"I'm just tired," she said. "Nothing to worry about."

Tim started to say something else but apparently thought better of it and left to go work in the yard. The evening passed quietly, and Rachel fell into bed, but again slept poorly. When she woke up the next morning she sensed she had just about reached the end of her rope. Something had to give.

After a quick breakfast with Tim, she hauled Kara to a soccer game, watched her play, then drove her home and left her with Tim. At Mixon's, visiting Ava, she hoped once more that Ava would recognize her, snap out of the Alzheimer's, and answer the questions that had plagued her since Mother's Day: Why did she have this affair with David Thorton? Could her mother actually have stumbled so? And how . . . how hypocritical it was for her to tell Rachel to keep herself pure, when she had done nothing of the sort in her own youth.

And what about Thorton? What kind of man was he? Obviously he was as big a hypocrite as Ava—worse really. At least Ava had not run from her actions. She had given birth to her daughter instead of hiding her shame with an abortion. Maybe Ava had yielded to the sin of sex before marriage, but she hadn't compounded it by shirking her duties as a mother.

Rachel fed Ava her lunch and looked into her eyes like a gold miner looking for a vein of the precious metal in a dark cave. She talked to her on and off for almost two hours. Ava, her hair loose on her shoulders, swallowed most of the food but showed no sign of seeing or hearing anything.

"Why did you tell me?" Rachel asked as she wiped her

momma's chin. "I had put it all behind me."

Ava stared into the corner. Rachel sighed. "I don't understand," she said. "What am I supposed to do now?"

Ava scratched her nose. Rachel laid the napkin on the tray by the bed. "You told me for a reason," she said. "I've just got to find out what that reason is."

Ava licked her lips. Rachel left her a few minutes later, her mind churning.

That afternoon she showed a young couple from Knoxville three different pieces of land where they might build a house, but her heart wasn't in it, and the couple drove away with no sign that they would make a purchase any time soon. But Rachel didn't care. Right now, her work mattered little to her, no more than something to pass the time until she . . . until she . . . until she what? That was the question, wasn't it? And she had no clue how to answer it.

At supper that night, she slumped at the table, her face sagging, her eyes dull. Nobody said much as they ate, and Kara left the table to watch television only a few minutes after they started. Rachel stood to take away the plates, but Tim caught her gently by the wrist and pulled her down to his lap. At first Rachel tried to pull away, but he wrapped his arms around her and held her still.

"Tell me what's going on," he said softly.

"Nothing," she said. "I'm just worn out."

He kissed her on the neck. "I don't doubt that," he said. "Hard as you work. But there's something else too. You're not yourself the last couple of weeks. I know you're not sleeping well . . . and you've lost weight too, something you don't need to do."

Rachel rose from his lap, and this time he let her go. She poured a glass of tea. Should she tell him, she wondered? But what could he do about it? Nothing, that's what. She drank from the tea. Tim stood and moved to the window, looked out a couple of minutes. He turned back to her.

"I know you had to put your Momma in Mixon's," he said. "And I can understand how hard it was. But you had no choice, you said that yourself."

Rachel drank again from her tea. Tim chewed at a thumbnail for a second. "We could move," he said. "Get a bigger place, let her live with us there."

Rachel set the tea on the table, walked to Tim and took his hands. "I appreciate your willingness to do that," she said. "But it won't solve what I'm dealing with."

He searched her face, concern etched in his big eyes. "I'll do whatever you want," he said. "You know that."

Rachel squeezed his hands. He was so good to her, a dream man really. He managed a thriving business but didn't let his job keep him from other things he enjoyed—hunting and fishing, watching Kara's soccer games, serving as a treasurer at their church. He had a quiet wisdom about him, and people responded to it by giving him responsibilities that only the trusted received. She wished more than once that she had a measure of his calm, the easy way he approached life.

"Momma told me something," she said, suddenly deciding to tell him about the encounter, at least part of it.

"What do you mean?" he asked.

"On Mother's Day," she said. "The day before I moved her to Mixon's."

Tim's eyebrows met in the middle, his confusion evident.

Rachel led him to the table, sat him down, and took the seat beside him. "It was out of nowhere," she said. "Momma, well, she woke up, that's the only way I know to describe it."

Tim studied her but said nothing. Rachel laid her palms flat on the table. Here it was. Time to say it out loud. "She told me who my father is," she said.

Tim rocked backward. "She what?"

"Told me the name of my father."

Quiet fell on the kitchen. Rachel watched Tim as her words soaked into his head. "I don't understand," he said. "Either part of it."

Rachel nodded. "I don't either," she said. "But Momma came back. A doctor in Asheville told me it happens sometimes, not often, but . . . well, it happened to Ava. And she told me my father's name. Not conscious more than ten minutes, but she gave me the name and then blanked out again."

Tim took her tea glass and drank from it. She almost laughed. Tim never drank tea.

"I know it sounds crazy," said Rachel. "But it's true. You know I wouldn't say it if it wasn't."

Tim placed the glass on the table. "You know I have to ask," he said.

"I don't know if I can tell you," Rachel said.

"Somebody I know?" asked Tim.

"Nope."

Tim stood and walked to the window. "What are you going to do about it?" he asked, gazing out.

"Don't know yet; that's why I hadn't told you."

He faced her, his hands in the pockets of his blue jeans. "You plan on meeting the man?"

"Not sure," she said. "Trying to figure it all out."

He moved to her, put his hands on her shoulders, massaging her neck. "It was a long time ago," he said. "Maybe it doesn't matter anymore."

Rachel closed her eyes. "Maybe you're right," she said. "But Momma told me for a reason. She said that's why she came back."

Tim's hands stilled. "Maybe she didn't know what she was saying. Not exactly clear headed these last few years."

Rachel stiffened. Though she knew Tim might be right, she didn't like hearing it. And for some reason she couldn't completely identify, she knew Ava hadn't been confused. Her message had come almost from beyond her, like she had no choice but to say it, like she was a messenger sent with an oracle from above.

"You know I have to ask his name," said Tim, his fingers busy on her neck again.

"I don't think I'm going to tell you," Rachel said. "At least not yet."

"You think I shouldn't know?" he asked.

"I'm trying to decide," she said. "Trying to decide a lot of things."

Tim's fingers pressed into her flesh, and she tried to relax into his touch. But her mind kept wandering to David Thorton, and by the time Kara walked back into the kitchen and Tim's massage ended, she had become angry at Thorton again. How dare he get off completely free from his actions; live like a king with no concern for his past sins. That wasn't the way the world should work, at least not her world.

Rachel stood and started to clean the table. As she did, she suddenly knew what she had to do, realized what she had been edging closer and closer to doing all week. She had to meet Thorton. That was the only way to put this whole thing behind her: meet him and deal with everything, do it no matter the consequences in her life or his. ❧

# CHAPTER SIX

# *Confrontations*

IT TOOK RACHEL UNTIL THURSDAY TO FIGURE OUT HOW AND when she wanted to meet Thorton. Don't go to his office and just announce it, she decided; and not to his house either, at least not at a time when she might run into his wife. No reason to unnecessarily upset anybody. In spite of his callous disregard for her all these years, she would not respond with deliberate cruelty. On Thursday morning, she sat down at her office desk and wrote a short letter.

> *Dear Mr. Thorton,*
>
> *I believe you know Mrs. Ava Wilson Robertson. I know her also; she is my momma. I believe you and I need to meet so we might talk about her and other related matters. Please call me on Monday morning at 704-885-2100. My name is Rachel Robertson Tyler.*

After signing her name, Rachel read the letter once more, then folded and sealed it in an envelope. Addressing the envelope to Thorton's address at Hendersonville High, she marked it "Personal and Confidential" and dropped it in the mail.

That night she slept well for the first time since Mother's Day. The simple act of making contact with Thorton relaxed her, made her feel she had rounded a corner, taken the first step toward some goal she had not yet fully identified.

Tim noticed the change the next morning, commenting at breakfast on the fact that she had not tossed and turned all night.

"You're feeling better," he said, more a statement really than a question.

Rachel sipped her coffee and nodded.

"You've decided what you want to do?"

Rachel started to tell him she was going to meet Thorton, then decided against it. Let it wait until she knew more, she figured, until she had met Thorton face to face.

"I'm dealing with it," she said.

Tim ate some toast. "You let me know if I can do anything," he said.

Rachel took his hand. Tim truly loved her. She appreciated him for that. "I'm going to be okay," she said. "Just dealing with a few issues."

Tim grinned. "Everybody's got some issues."

"Even you?"

"Everybody but me," he said. "I'm a puppy, remember?"

Rachel laughed for the first time in what seemed like forever. Tim laughed too, and as the sound of it filled the room, Rachel thought for just an instant that maybe she could make it through this—make it through and find some peace on the other side.

∞∞∞

At four minutes past eight a.m. the next Monday, the phone rang at Rachel's desk at the office of Blue Ridge Realty. A coffee cup in hand, she stared at the phone for a second as if it might rise up at any second and bite her. It rang a second time. Her hands quivered, and she almost dropped the coffee cup. But then, before a third ring, she picked up the phone.

"Mrs. Rachel Tyler please." The voice sounded important, like a preacher or a radio personality.

"This is Mrs. Tyler." She carefully placed her coffee on the desk and looked around as if to make sure nobody heard her.

"David Thorton here. I received your letter."

He sounded guarded, but Rachel had expected as much. "Thank you for calling," she said. It sounded dumb, but she didn't know what else to say.

"You said you wanted to talk," said Thorton, moving directly to the point.

Rachel switched the phone to her left ear and turned her back to the rest of the office. "I do," she said. "But not on the phone. In person."

She heard him sigh. It sounded weary, like a man who had tried to keep a dangerous animal trapped for a long time but who now had to deal with the fact that his prey had escaped. Rachel's temper surged, and she squeezed the phone harder.

"I've expected this for a long time," said Thorton.

"Excuse me?" She didn't know if she liked his statement or not.

"You can come to my house," said Thorton.

That surprised her. "You think that's wise?" she asked.

"My wife is out of town," he said. "Can you come today? The sooner we do this the better. About five maybe?"

Rachel considered the situation. Tim didn't expect her until about seven. She had an appointment at 5:30 that she could re-schedule. Why not go today? Face the matter without any more delay. A combination of thrill and dread rushed through her.

"I'll be there," she said.

"I assume you know where I live," he said.

"I do."

"Then I'll see you at five." He hung up.

Rachel did likewise and glanced around the office. Two other real estate agents were on phones at desks across the room. A secretary stood at a copy machine. Stacks of paper rested on every desk. Sun streamed through the front window. The smell of coffee drifted in the air like a cloud. Everything seemed the same. The people were busy at their jobs as if the world had not just shifted under their feet. But Rachel knew different. She picked up her coffee. But her hands shook so badly she needed both of them around the cup to make sure she didn't spill it all over the papers on her desk.

∝∽∾

At four minutes until five, Rachel steered her pickup into David Thorton's driveway and switched it off. For a couple of minutes she sat still as a statue, her mind clicking in a thousand directions. She hadn't told Tim about this meeting. For one thing, she hadn't talked to him all day, and for another she didn't want to bother him with all this if not necessary. Until she knew what this all meant, it made no sense to get Tim involved.

A soft breeze played with her hair as she checked herself in the rear view mirror. Make-up okay, hair fine, eyes tired but not too bad. She almost laughed. What did it matter what she looked like? This wasn't a job interview or a client. She sucked in a deep breath. This was more important. This was the first time she had ever met her biological father, the first time he had seen her. Her hand tingled as she re-adjusted the mirror. No matter what happened next, her life had changed. She felt like a teenager again, scared and anxious.

With her teeth clenched against the quivering in her stomach, she opened the door and stepped to the sidewalk. A bird chirped in an oak tree to her left, but she didn't notice. One foot in front of the other, one foot in front of the other. Her eyes set on the lines in the sidewalk, she paid no attention to anything, not the bees busy at the flowers by the walk, not the breeze playing in her hair, not the thumping of her heart so heavy it sounded like a bass drum in her ears. Step, step, step all the way to David Thorton's door.

On the front stoop, she hesitated and licked her lips. She almost turned around and ran back to the truck. But then she reminded herself that she, Rachel Robertson Tyler, didn't run from anything—never had, never would. To leave now cut against every fiber of her being, every muscle, every hair, every organ, every chromosome in her body. She was no quitter, and she would not let David Thorton turn her into one.

Her chin set, she raised a finger and jabbed the doorbell. Thorton arrived before she touched it a second time. One second she stood on the stoop all alone. The next second the man who had fathered her stood within two feet of her face, his dimpled chin and brown eyes so similar to hers she felt her knees weaken. Thorton stuck out a thick hand. For an instant, Rachel stared at the hand as if watching a snake preparing for a strike. But when Thorton made no threatening moves, she relented and took his hand. His skin felt warm but not overly so.

"I'm David Thorton," he said. "Welcome to my home."

Rachel dropped his hand and studied him for a couple of seconds: khaki slacks, blue shirt, brown loafers; about five ten, broad like a block of ice; silver gray hair, small ears but sprigged out of the sides of his head—like hers.

"Rachel Tyler," she finally said, knowing she couldn't stare at him forever. "Thank you for inviting me."

Thorton stepped back to let her enter. Rachel tried to read his face for some clue to his feelings, but she couldn't tell a thing. Inside the house, the two faced each other for several more seconds. But then Rachel broke off the eye contact and gazed around the house.

"This is a beautiful place," she said, her voice weaker than she wanted.

"I know," he said. "My wife has wonderful taste."

Rachel surveyed the entryway. A deep, hand-woven rug lay under her feet. Hardwood floors stretched out past the rug. A chandelier at least four feet across hung from a high ceiling. Several pieces of antique furniture sat in the living room to the right, and a dining room table, side buffet, and china hutch rested in a dining room to the left. The furnishings weren't the most impressive part of what she saw, though. Pictures of Thorton's family hung everywhere: playing games, eating, swimming, laughing here at Christmas and there on birthdays, graduating from school, going to a dance—you name it, the Thorton's had a picture of it on the wall. A lot like Ava and the pictures in her bedroom—well, her former bedroom.

"My passion," said Thorton, noting her interest in the pictures. "I'm a bit of a photographer."

"More than a bit," said Rachel, genuinely impressed. "These are good."

Thorton shrugged. "I enjoy doing it," he said. "Especially with the family."

A surge of jealousy ran through Rachel's spine. Anger too. Thorton loved his family, no doubt about it. At least part of it, anyway. Before she could stop herself, she heard her voice. "I have been told you are my father," she said.

Thorton rubbed his chin. "That I am," he said.

"You don't deny it?" asked Rachel, surprised at his quick acceptance of a fact he had hidden for years.

He shook his head, looking squarely at her. "Nope, no denial, none at all. I've been waiting on this day for a long time."

Rachel couldn't tell if he was expressing grief or gladness that the day had finally arrived.

"Come on," he said. "Let's sit down and have us a talk."

Not knowing what else to do, Rachel followed him into a large den. He motioned her to a navy leather chair by a stone fireplace. She took the seat, soaking in the décor as she did: A leather sofa to match the chair, a fireplace from floor to ceiling, a large round window overlooking a back yard filled with trees. As in the entryway, family pictures adorned all the walls.

Thorton took a chair similar to hers by the sofa and examined her as if inspecting a creature that no one had ever seen.

"You're petite," he said. "Like Ava."

Rachel's tongue stuck to the bottom of her mouth.

"I'm sorry Ava has not been well," said Thorton.

His awareness startled Rachel into speech. "You know about her?" she asked.

Thorton shifted. "I know she's in the nursing home."

Rachel rubbed her hands together, trying to collect herself.

Thorton knew more than she expected, and that knocked her off balance. Knowledge gave people the upper hand, any real estate agent knew that. She cleared her throat and changed the subject. "When will your wife return?" she asked.

"Not until tomorrow."

"We have a lot to talk about," said Rachel.

Thorton picked a golf ball out of a bowl by his chair, rolled it in his hand. "I expect we do," he said. "You want to go first or shall I?"

"Why don't you begin?" said Rachel. "You seem to know more than I do." She hoped he noted her slightly sarcastic tone.

"Where shall I start?" he asked, friendly as ever.

Rachel chewed her lip. The golf ball in Thorton's hand bothered her. He seemed so relaxed about everything. Not exactly the posture she expected—or wanted—from him. She preferred to see some anxiety, something to show he recognized what she could do to him, how she could hurt him, hurt him like he had hurt her.

"Begin with you and Momma," she said, deciding to dispense with any small talk and move to the heart of the matter. "Tell me about the two of you."

Thorton dropped his eyes for a second. "You don't mess around do you?"

"No time for it," said Rachel, glad to see his discomfort.

"Okay." Thorton placed the golf ball back in the bowl and leaned forward. Rachel caught her breath. Was he really going to tell her? Tell her what she had wanted to know since the awful day of her eighteenth birthday?

"It's not a pretty picture," said Thorton.

"Just say it," said Rachel. "I've waited long enough."

Thorton rubbed his face. "Okay," he said. "You know that Ava's pa had a drinking problem."

Rachel shrugged. She knew that part of the story. Her grand-daddy Wilson died at sixty-three years, a man of giant sized appetites for food and liquor; a man who argued loudly and threw his weight around like a large boulder ready to crush anybody who stood in his way.

"Theodore Wilson treated your grandma rough," said Thorton. "Rougher than any man ought to treat a woman."

Rachel wanted to tell Thorton that he had no room to speak on such an issue, but she bit her tongue. No use making this any more unpleasant than it already was.

Thorton continued. "Wilson came from the old school. Believed a woman should bow down to a man."

"What's that got to do with me?" interrupted Rachel. "Granddad and Grandma are both dead, almost fifteen years ago now."

Thorton stood and trudged to the window, his hands in his pockets. "He treated his kids rough too," he said. "Your momma and her two brothers."

Rachel tensed. Thorton knew things about her family that Ava had never told her. "How come Momma never told me any of this?" she asked, suddenly suspicious that Thorton might be making this up to make himself look better. He faced her.

"You know Ava," he said. "Didn't like to dwell on the nega-tive. Always stressed the bright side of things."

Rachel smiled slightly. What Thorton said was true. Her momma could step in a pile of horse manure and be glad because it meant a pony must be around somewhere.

"I think she protected herself that way," Thorton continued. "Kept her mind off the bad things. Later, she shifted that trait over to her dealings with you and your brothers. Told you mostly the good stuff, hiding the rest deep in her soul."

"So her dad treated her mean," said Rachel, her emotions a touch softer but still wanting Thorton to tell how all this affected her.

"Yeah," he said. "Real mean. Ava and I started dating right after she turned sixteen. But her pa didn't want her dating me, or anybody else for that matter."

"Most dads are like that," said Rachel, thinking of Tim and the way he sometimes teased that Kara couldn't date until she turned twenty-one.

Thorton smiled. "I know," he said. "I've got a grown daughter myself. But Wilson . . . well, he took it to extremes. Gave Ava piles of chores on Friday and Saturday night that she had to finish before we could go out. And he made her come home by 10:30, and punished her if she missed the curfew by even five minutes or so."

Thorton shoved his hands deeper into his pockets. "I remember this one time," he said. "We were driving home from a high school football game. Everybody in town had attended, Theodore Wilson included. On the way home we drove up on a three-car accident. One of Ava's friends was in one of the cars. We stopped like everybody else. Couldn't do anything but stop. The road was blocked in both directions."

Thorton moved away from the window, leaned on the fireplace, and looked at the floor for a second. "Ava saw her friend lying on the side of the road," he continued. "Ran to her. Her friend looked up, called her name. Ava sat down, took her friend's head in her lap. Blood was everywhere."

Thorton inhaled as if trying to suck all the air in the room into his lungs. Rachel realized she was holding her breath. Thorton spoke again, his tone soft. "Ava's pa had left the game about halfway through the fourth quarter. Was already home by the time the wreck happened. But Ava and I were an hour and a half late. Her friend died on the road while she held her."

Thorton's eyes watered. "When we walked into Ava's house, I knew immediately that her pa had hit the bottle pretty hard. The house smelled like a brewery, and his face was all red and puffy, almost as red as the blood covering the front of Ava's sweater from where her friend had bled on her."

"What happened?" whispered Rachel.

Thorton grunted. "Wilson went nuts. Threw a clock at us. Screamed at Ava that she was nothing but plain loose, that she had no shame, that he was embarrassed to be her daddy. Ava tried to show him the blood on her sweater. She told him about the accident . . . her friend dying."

"He didn't believe her?"

Thorton laughed. "I'm sure he did," he said. "But it didn't matter. We were late, death or no death."

"Where was her momma?"

Thorton shrugged. "Not home that night. Her own momma had some health problems. She stayed with her some, maybe to get away from Wilson. Who knows? But she wasn't there."

Rachel hated to ask but knew she must. "What did Granddad do to Momma?"

Thorton pressed both hands against the sides of his head as if he could squeeze out the memory. Then he shook his head at Rachel as if he didn't want to speak it out.

"What did he do?" Rachel repeated.

Thorton moved to the window again, stared out as if hoping he could see a way to answer that would make it all better, all different. "He made her stay home," he said. "For the next two weeks. Other than school and church, she went nowhere . . . and I do mean nowhere."

Rachel's heart stopped momentarily. Thorton faced her again. "Nowhere," he repeated. "Not even to the funeral for the friend who died in her lap."

For several minutes the room fell quiet. A clock bonged in the front hallway. Rachel stood and moved to the window by Thorton.

"I can see you loved her," she said. "So why didn't you marry her? Why did you get her in trouble and then leave her?"

Though Rachel didn't say it out loud, she wanted to speak of herself too, to ask David Thorton why he had run off from both her and her momma. But then she answered her own question. Thorton had left Ava precisely because of her. The fact of her embryonic existence ran him off in the first place. If not for her, he might have eventually married Ava, married her and protected her from the shame and suffering she later endured.

Rachel's anger boiled up again at this conclusion and she wanted to strike out at this man who had used her momma for his own pleasure but then skipped out when the pleasure ended and the duties of marriage and parenthood beckoned. She started to pivot, to leave David Thorton forever. She had survived without him all these years, nothing to keep her from doing so for the rest of her life. But then she saw a smile flicker across his face, a smile tempered with an unspoken grief.

"You really don't know, do you?" he asked.

"Know what?"

"Come with me," he said. "Let me show you something." ❧

*Although the world is full of*

*suffering, it is also full of the*

*overcoming of it.*

HELEN KELLER

❖❖❖

# CHAPTER SEVEN

# *Revelations*

THOUGH STILL UPSET, RACHEL FOUND IT IMPOSSIBLE TO LEAVE
David Thorton's house. As if held in place by the talons of the
devil himself, she felt compelled to follow him. After leading
her from the den, he turned left and opened a door that led
down a set of steps to a basement. Without speaking, Thorton
gestured toward the basement and Rachel nodded dumbly.
Whatever he had in mind, she had come too far to back out
now.

They eased down the stairs and turned right. The basement
had a concrete floor and a row of overhead lights that
hummed as she passed under them. Thorton moved through a
game room filled with a pool table, a television and enough
bean bag chairs to fill a college dormitory. Rachel followed.
Beyond the game room, they reached a wooden door on the
right. The door was locked.

"My study," said Thorton. "My kids used to call it 'Dad's
Dungeon.'"

A sudden flash of fear rolled through Rachel. A dungeon
sounded dangerous. Thorton unlocked the door before she
could think of an excuse to leave. He edged back to let her
enter. Her nerves on alert, she moved by him into the room.

No more than twelve by thirteen, the study was filled with a wall of book shelves, a small metal desk and two chairs—a black leather one behind the desk and a wood one in front. Hardwood covered the floor and pictures of Thorton's family covered all the walls but the one with the shelves. Two cameras perched on the edge of the desk, their lenses out like a pair of eyes ready to take a shot at anything that moved.

Rachel twisted slowly in a full circle. Pictures, pictures, pictures. To the left, to the right, behind and in front. Just like upstairs. Facing Thorton again, Rachel said, "No doubt about it, you're a real family man." She hoped he caught her sarcasm.

Apparently taking no offense, Thorton sat down on the corner of the desk nearest her, picked up one of the cameras and rolled it around in his hands. "I can tell you're upset," he said. "And I'm sorry for that."

Rachel grunted. His gentle spirit made her even madder. How dare he appear so nice? So willing to talk? Didn't he know she could ruin him? Tear up this family that he had hung all over the walls? Didn't he realize she could destroy his squeaky clean reputation? Yet he treated her like no threat at all.

She ground her teeth. She would not let him handle her, steer her away from her fury. "You've made a nice home for yourself and your family," she said, not bothering to hide the threat. "Pillar of the community and all that."

Thorton placed the camera on the desk, studied his shoes, the heels worn down on the outer edges. Odd, thought Rachel, she wore her shoes out in an identical pattern. Her anger rose even more.

"I know you hate me right now," said Thorton. "And I can understand—"

"You don't understand anything!" interrupted Rachel, her

fists balled, her scorn boiling over. "You put my mother in a family way and then bailed out on her—left her all alone to have a baby. That baby was me! Momma raises me, takes on all the shame, all the snide remarks from the high and mighty. Then, all these years, we live in the next town. Surely you know that, but you do nothing to help us. And what are you doing all that time? Well . . . you're building a snug little place for yourself, acting like a man of faith, all spit and polish, a regular spiritual giant. What a laugh!"

She finished her tirade and fell into the wood chair, suddenly weary from the verbal outpouring.

"It's not what you think," said Thorton. "Not by a long way."

Rachel shook her head. "Don't defend yourself," she said. "You're nothing more than a hypocrite!"

Thorton rubbed his face with both hands, then stood and walked to a small door in the wall to the left of the desk. Opening the door, he motioned for Rachel to follow him inside. Though exasperated by his measured response to everything, she saw no option but to see this to the end. She'd let Thorton defend himself however he wanted then wash her hands of him forever.

Out of the chair, she eased across the room, ducked slightly through the small door and entered a room approximately half the size of the outer office. A single recessed light burned in the ceiling, and the place smelled like a wet shoe. A safe— about three feet high and two feet wide—sat in the center of the room.

As quiet as a sphinx, Thorton squatted before the safe and slipped a key into a front lock. A second later, he opened the safe and pulled out four folders, each of them stuffed.

On his feet again, Thorton pointed her to the one chair in the room, a straight-backed hard chair beside the safe. Though completely mystified, Rachel took the seat. Thorton handed her the four folders.

"Take a look at these," he said.

She glanced at the folders and then back up at Thorton.

"Go ahead," he said. "Nothing in there will bite you."

Curious in spite of herself, Rachel pulled a paper clip off the first folder, opened it and poured the contents into her lap. Her eyes widened. She looked back at Thorton, her brow furrowed.

"Go ahead," he said. "Take a good look."

Pictures. A folder full of pictures. But not just any pictures. Pictures of her! She recognized many of them because Ava had copies in her own belongings!

As if handling an explosive, Rachel held the pictures up one by one and studied them. They were all taken after Ava moved with her back to Rock Branch.

The pictures chronicled her life. Pictures of her after she lost her first tooth. Pictures of her the first day of first grade. Pictures of her early birthdays. Pictures the Christmas she turned seven and eight.

More confused than ever, she faced Thorton. "Momma gave you pictures of me?" she asked, not willing to consider the other explanation.

He laughed slightly and shook his head. "Try the next folder," he suggested. "I believe they're numbered."

They were. Rachel opened the one with the "two" on it. More pictures. Only she was older now. Nine, ten, eleven, twelve, thirteen. Playing the piano at a recital. Receiving baptism at the Methodist Church. With a black eye from the time a softball hit her in the face.

Studying the pictures closely, she noticed something different about them from the earlier ones. These were taken from a further distance and none from inside her house.

Unable to deny what he had done, she stared at Thorton for several seconds. Who was he?

"I suppose I'll find more pictures in the other two folders?" she asked, staring at Thorton.

He nodded. "Yes. Like the day you went on your first date at sixteen. You looked so beautiful in your jeans, a dark green blouse I believe it was, a necklace with a cross, earrings to match, only not the dangling kind."

"And the shoes?"

Thorton shrugged. "I never could remember shoes. Don't know why."

Rachel quickly thumbed through the third and fourth folders. Both contained pictures—images from practically every major event in her life. The night the school voted her homecoming queen, her speech as valedictorian, walking the stage at college graduation, even one from her wedding.

As she fingered the pictures, a wall of tears welled up, but they weren't tears of joy as she might have expected. The tears felt hot instead, as hot as boiling water, hot and angry. David Thorton had watched her, spied on her as if she were some kind of circus animal, something to see but never contact, something to observe but never encounter. She felt violated, as if he had stalked her. Through his camera Thorton had invaded her life without revealing a clue about his. How much he must know about her, things she didn't want him to know, things he had no right to know!

Before she could stop herself, she lashed out, her face almost a snarl. "You think this means something?" she snapped, holding up the folders as if to threaten him with them. "You took some pictures. Big deal! You do this to make yourself feel better, allow yourself to say you're involved in your daughter's life. I mean, hey, you're watching your little girl, surely she knows you love her because of that! Snapping a few pictures proves what a good man you are, how you're thinking about her, checking on her."

She paused for a second but not long enough for him to interrupt. "But what about my momma all that time? The way she struggled to make ends meet. Especially in the early years before she married Ray, then later when he died. What about then?"

Rachel stood now and moved closer to Thorton. For a second she thought she might hit him, throw her fists into his chest and pound away at his impassive flesh. But she caught herself before that happened and stood still as a statue, her fists clenched around the folders, her face flushed. Thorton had still not responded, and she knew why. He had no defense, nothing to say. She shouted at him now, her voice bouncing off the walls of the tiny room.

"She worked all her life! Put me through college, the three boys too." Sarcasm dripped from her lips. "But hey, you took pictures! How noble! How responsible! How . . . how loving!"

Rachel threw the folders to the floor. A cascade of pictures tumbled out and splashed across the hardwood, several of them sliding under the safe. Tears filled Rachel's eyes, and she twisted around the room, looking for the door, searching for the way to escape. Stepping over the pictures, she moved toward the door. But Thorton grabbed her elbow and held her in place, his thick fingers firm but not abusive.

"What are you going to do?" he asked.

Rachel almost spat at him. "You're afraid I'll go to your wife, aren't you?" she asked. "Kick down this little house of cards you've built for yourself."

Thorton let her go and shoved his hands into his pockets. "That's not it," he said. "Not at all. Louise has known about my relationship with Ava since the day I asked Louise to marry me. She has known about you too, since the first I learned of your birth."

Rachel's mouth fell open, and her feet stuck to the floor. Thorton studied his shoes. "I would never keep this kind of secret from my wife. It's true my kids don't know, but that's because . . . well . . . I didn't want to take a chance that they might interfere with your life. You seemed okay, and I thought it might hurt you more than anything else. So I just haven't told them. But I will. I'm not afraid of it."

Rachel stared at the pictures on the floor. Thorton had surprised her again. Her earlier drive to leave melted away. "Your wife knows about me?"

"Sure. And Ava knew I took the pictures."

"What?" Rachel's surprise turned to shock.

"Ava knew," he said. "Ray too. Remember the earlier pictures? Some were taken inside your house."

Rachel wracked her brain to remember any previous contact with Thorton. Nothing came to her.

"I stayed real low key," said Thorton. "No reason for you to suspect anything."

Rachel calmed just a little. But not enough to forgive him for anything. Okay, the man had taken some pictures. That proved nothing. He had provided no help to Ava. He was a jerk and nothing in the pictures changed that.

Thorton moved to the chair by the safe, pointing Rachel to it. "Here, sit again," he said. "I need to show you something else."

Wondering if the surprises would ever end, Rachel parked in the chair once more. By the safe again, Thorton pulled out a handful of envelopes. As with the folders, he handed them to Rachel, then stepping back to give her space to consider the new evidence in her hands.

∞∞∞

"Checks," Rachel said a few minutes later when she had finished going through the envelopes.

"I know," said Thorton, perched on the edge of the safe, a touch of a smile on his lips. "I wrote them."

Rachel looked back through the stack of canceled checks in her lap. All of them were written on an account from the First Municipal Bank of Hendersonville. And all of them had been written to pay for something she had needed. Checks to buy school clothes; checks to pay for braces; checks for her homecoming dress and shoes; checks for college tuition.

Her head in her hands, Rachel tried to calm down. It made no sense. But apparently David Thorton had involved himself far deeper in her life than she had ever imagined. Not only had he watched her and taken pictures, but he had also financially supported her almost from the beginning.

"I wanted to help any way I could," he said softly. "I loved you more than you'll ever know. Tried to do my part, even if from a distance. I wanted to make sure you and Ava had enough to make it."

Rachel stared at Thorton as if seeing an alien from some far distant planet. But she was not angry now, just utterly confused.

"I've tried to think of it like God might," Thorton said. "You know, your children don't always know you're there, but you are. You're watching them like God watches us, keeping an eye on what happens, ready to step in if necessary."

Rachel rubbed her thumbs over the checks. Thorton made so much sense. He had watched over her, even when she didn't know it.

"I tried to provide too," Thorton continued. "Like God often does even when we don't see it, don't know it's happening. Not that Ava would let me do as much as I wanted. But I did help, especially when you needed it most, after Ray died, when you and Ava were so alone, when she was hurting so much, when you went off to school so confused, so confused about . . . about . . ."

Rachel looked back up. Thorton seemed so sincere, so caring. But . . . but wait! He couldn't buy her off this easily. Just because he took a few pictures, wrote some checks from a bank account that obviously had plenty in it. None of that caused any real sacrifice on his part. None of it made up for his desertion of Ava, the way she had to bear all the shame, all the guilt of delivering a fatherless child. And, maybe worse for her, no matter what Thorton did or said, his lack of courage had made her a bastard, a child without a father.

A sudden revelation surged through Rachel—an insight so obvious that she marveled that she could have lived so long without seeing it. But now that she saw it, her anger at Thorton reached a fevered pitch.

Since the day she turned eighteen, she had labored with the knowledge of her illegitimacy. And now, for the first time, she saw that her drive—her compulsion really—to push herself, to prove she had value, had started that day. In all the years since she found out that Ray wasn't her daddy, she had struggled, even obsessed, over her identity. That had compelled her to strive harder, study longer hours, work more diligently—all in an effort to measure up with everybody else.

Finally aware of what had rested hidden just beneath the surface for years, Rachel focused her attention on Thorton once more. He had caused her to become "Rush It Rachel." His cowardice had created the empty space in her soul that nothing had ever filled, and she would not, indeed could not, forgive him for it.

She pushed quickly from the chair, shoved the envelopes at Thorton and fled from the room before he could react. Scrambling up the basement stairs, she heard him rushing to catch her.

"Hang on a second," he shouted. "We need to finish this!"

She rushed through the hallway. "It is finished!" she shouted as she reached the front door. "It's over!"

At the truck, she threw open the door and hopped in. Thorton ran toward her, his face red. For a second, a quiver of fear ran down her spine and she wondered again if he might hurt her to keep her from revealing his secret. But then she told herself to slow down, not let her imagination go off half-cocked. Even as bad as he was, Thorton had shown no tendency toward violence.

Regaining some calm, she flipped on the ignition. Thorton appeared at her window, but she refused to roll it down.

"I need to tell you one more thing!" shouted Thorton.

Rachel vigorously shook her head. She was done with David Thorton. Carefully, so as to avoid running over his feet, she backed out of the driveway, changed gears and sped away. In the rearview mirror, she saw Thorton, his hands in his pockets, shuffling back to his house. ❧

# CHAPTER EIGHT

*Openings*

FOR ALMOST A WEEK, RACHEL TRIED TO TELL HERSELF IT WAS over. She had met her father and, though he had flipped over a few cards she hadn't expected to see, none of that changed her feelings about him. No matter that he had snapped a few pictures and written a few checks—she was still a girl with no father. Though he said he loved her, she knew otherwise. A man who loves his daughter doesn't stay absent from her life, no matter the complications.

As usual when she felt anxious, Rachel focused on her job. But this time that failed her. Work had lost its zing. Whether somebody bought or did not buy a house or a piece of land meant about as much to her as whether she ate fried or scrambled eggs for breakfast. She just flat didn't care either way.

Like a zombie on downers, she slogged her way through the week—work, Mixon's nursing facility, home. Show a house, feed her momma, cook and clean for Kara and Tim. Finish one day and start another. Eyes blank, head down, sleep non-existent, appetite absent, body losing weight, words flat, energy low.

Tim asked her if she wanted to talk, but she said no, she just had some things to sort out. He, like always, left her alone. When visiting Ava, she said little, spooning food into her momma's mouth with no more interaction than a coffee machine dispensing a cup of hot drink to a half-asleep customer. Lost in the Alzheimer's, Ava said nothing and Rachel stopped wishing for anything different. For the first time in her life, she truly felt at a dead end—as boxed in as a horse in a corral, nowhere to turn, nowhere to run. Where before she had always believed she could do something to improve a bad situation, she felt no such hope this time. To make matters worse, she now realized that all her accomplishments had not changed what she had felt about herself since that fateful eighteenth birthday. None of her achievements altered what she was. She understood that now, and that knocked away every prop she had ever trusted. Without the props of her accolades and the applause they earned, she felt naked, a person in a prison of low esteem and self-loathing.

The week concluded, and Sunday morning dawned. Rachel claimed a cold and refused to leave the bed. Gentle as always, Tim encouraged her to stay put. "You need some rest," he said, giving her a quick peck on the cheek as he headed to the shower. "You just stay here. I'll take Kara to church. We'll see you about 12:30."

Though feeling guilty, Rachel had no energy to join them. "I'll be okay with a bit more sleep," she said. "I'll get up in an hour or so, fix some lunch. We'll eat together when you two come home."

"Just take care of yourself," said Tim.

Forty-five minutes later, Kara gave her a kiss and left with Tim for church. Alone in the quiet house, Rachel stayed in bed for almost another hour. Outside her window, the sun rose higher. Her face warmed as fingers of light reached through the drapes. Unable to stay put any longer, Rachel pushed back her hair and climbed out of bed. After brushing her teeth and hair and slipping into a bathrobe, she made her way to the kitchen, poured a cup of coffee and moved to the kitchen table. A vase filled with fresh yellow roses sat on the table, and her spirits momentarily rose a notch as she thought of Kara or Tim cutting them. But then she picked up the newspaper Tim had left by the vase and saw a front-page story detailing how five different families planned to spend Father's Day.

Rachel slammed the paper down. Father's Day! She had completely forgotten! What kind of wife was she? Or mother either for that matter? She had let Tim and Kara leave for church and she hadn't said a word. Was he mad at her? No doubt of that. He ought to be furious. She had become so focused on her own issues that she had totally ignored anything else. She was a selfish person—a terrible wife and mother.

Her spirits as low as she could ever remember, Rachel headed back to bed. Might as well give in to the depression and let it soak her like a bleak rain. Halfway down the hall, the doorbell ring. She hesitated, but then decided to see who it was. She kept walking. The bell rang again. She turned and moved to the door. Through the front windows she saw a man's body, but the drapes obscured his face. Who in the world?

A salesman, she figured, though most salesmen didn't visit on Sunday mornings. Tying her robe tighter at the waist, she opened the door. Her breath caught. David Thorton stood on her front porch, his gray suit matching his hair, his shoes shined so well you could see your face in them. Rachel started to slam the door, but Thorton shoved a shoe between it and the wall and stopped her.

"I need just a couple of minutes," he said.

She didn't move. Thorton pulled his foot back. She left the door open. If he had come this far, she might as well give him his two minutes. Thorton shoved his hands into his pockets. Rachel stayed quiet. Though she hadn't run him off, she wasn't about to make this easy. Thorton cleared his throat. "Look," he said. "I'm sorry to bother you, but I've been sitting over there —" he pointed to an empty lot across the street, "for close to two hours. Watched your husband and daughter leave some time ago. Have been trying to muster up my nerve."

"I see you managed to do so," said Rachel, finally finding her voice.

Thorton looked back at his shoes.

"I'm not feeling well," said Rachel, not sure what else to say.

Thorton glanced back up, caught her eyes, and locked in. "I'm not feeling well either," he said. "But it's not a physical ailment."

"Life is tough," said Rachel. She knew she was squeezing him, but saw no reason to do anything else. So let him stand there and feel uncomfortable. She had felt that way for years, ill at ease, out of place, uncomfortable in a world where everybody except her knew their roots.

"It's Father's Day," said Thorton.

Rachel gave a chuckle, but it had no joy in it.

"And I am your father," Thorton continued.

"So I hear."

"I told you last week we needed to finish this," he said. "But what I should have said was we needed to start it."

"What do you mean?" Rachel wished she hadn't sounded so interested.

Thorton cleared his throat. "There's one more thing you need to know," he said.

"And what's that?"

"I need to show you," he said. "At my house."

"I'm not exactly dressed to go out," she said, indicating her bathrobe.

"I'll wait for you to change," said Thorton.

"You're serious, aren't you?"

"As serious as I've ever been about anything in my life."

Rachel's curiosity took over in spite of her misgivings. "What about your wife?" she asked.

"My wife knows I'm here. She went to church to pray for me."

"Understanding woman."

"You don't know the half of it."

Rachel considered the situation. No matter what Thorton showed her, it wouldn't change her mind about him. He was a hypocrite, nothing could alter that fact. So why not go with him? Let him play out his little show and tell. What harm could it do? Then she could move on with her life. She thought of Tim and Kara. They wouldn't come home for at least another hour. She studied Thorton for another second. Something important had pushed him to come here. If she didn't go with him, he might come back later and try to talk to Tim or something.

"Okay." She stepped back. "Why don't you come in while I change?" she said. "Take me about five minutes."

Thorton smiled. But Rachel saw no reason to join him. ✿

# CHAPTER NINE

# Secrets and Blessings

FORTY-FIVE MINUTES LATER, RACHEL PULLED INTO DAVID THORTON'S driveway, parked her truck behind his black sedan, and smoothed down the front of the blue jean skirt she had hurriedly slipped on. She felt weird and out of place. Yet she knew she had to go forward. No matter what, she had to see this to the finish. Resigned, she watched as Thorton stepped out of his car and motioned her to follow him. What a strange man, she thought. Though he had fathered an illegitimate child, he didn't seem at all defensive about it—not the least ashamed and not particularly bothered by her anger. She wondered why he had brought her here, what he thought he could show her that would make a difference in her feelings about him? Nothing, that's what. Absolutely nothing!

Thorton motioned again and shoved his hands into his pockets. Rachel's resentment boiled up once more, and she considered backing out of the driveway and leaving. But something made her stop. She had come this far. She might as well go the final step. She opened the door and climbed out. A few seconds later she followed Thorton into his house, down the basement steps, and into his office. Both of them were silent.

In his study, Thorton pointed her to the wooden chair. She took it, her eyes down. Thorton perched on the edge of his desk. His big shoes stretched toward her, his ankles crossed.

"I know you resent me right now," he said, his tone as even as a therapist trying to calm an angry client.

Rachel said nothing.

"I can't blame you," he said. "I wasn't there for you."

Still silence from Rachel.

"But it wasn't my choice," he said. "It was Ava's. That's the way she wanted it."

Rachel glanced up, not liking what she heard. "That's easy to say," she said, spitting out the words. "When she can't contradict you."

Thorton uncrossed his ankles, moved to the chair behind the desk, and sat down. "I don't expect you to believe me," he said. "But it's true. Ava refused to let me claim you as my daughter. She said it would just confuse everybody—you most of all."

Rachel almost laughed. Thorton had worked on his story since she last saw him. He now had a response in case she went public with her information. She folded her arms across her waist. "Let me get this straight," she said. "You're saying that Ava wouldn't let you tell people you were my father?"

"Exactly," he said. "She said she loved me too much to let me ruin my reputation, my future."

"But you didn't love her enough to keep her from ruining hers?"

Thorton noticeably slumped, and then he opened the middle drawer of his desk. "Ava said her reputation was ruined anyway, no matter what I did or didn't do. No way to hide the fact that she was pregnant."

"Pretty good for you, huh?"

Thorton reached into the drawer and pulled out something Rachel couldn't see. "Only five people know what really happened," he said. "My wife, your Momma, me, and Mr. and Mrs. Theodore Wilson."

"Two of those folks are dead, one is married to you, and the fourth has no ability to say anything to the contrary. Again, pretty good for you."

Thorton sighed heavily. "I've carried the guilt around for over forty years," he said. "The shame of not telling people I was your father, the shame of letting Ava deal with the pregnancy all alone, the shame of never coming to you . . . telling you that you had a daddy who loved you."

Rachel's fists clenched. What did Thorton know about shame? She's the one who had a bucket—no make that a truck load—of that to haul around, a load so heavy it threatened to crush her.

"I think we're done here," she said, standing up.

Thorton held up his hand, revealing a key. "I said I had something to show you," he said. "You mustn't leave until you see it."

"I believe I've seen enough," said Rachel, her head suddenly aching, her body weary.

"This is important," said Thorton. "To me . . . and to you."

Rachel heard the somber tones in his voice. She studied his face. It seemed genuine. Though still suspicious of a trick, she waved him to go ahead. One final thing. She would give him that. Then she would wash her hands of him forever.

Thorton moved to the door of the room that contained the safe. A couple of seconds later he reemerged, an envelope in his hand. Without a word, he handed her the envelope, then perched again on the desk. "Open the envelope," he said. "It's what I wanted you to see a week ago."

Almost flippantly, Rachel sat down, opened the envelope and slipped out the document inside. She caught her breath, her tongue glued to the roof of her mouth. It looked like a . . . like a wedding license!

She read it quickly, the names centered on it. David Russell Thorton. Ava Marie Wilson. The license said:

*"On this day of December 29, 1948, I, the Reverend Bruce Fanning, do hereby unite according to the laws of the state of North Carolina, David Russell Thorton and Ava Marie Wilson in the bonds of Holy Matrimony."*

Unable to believe it, Rachel read the line again. It came out the same the second time. She looked back at Thorton. Her mind reeled with all kinds of possibilities, but none of them made sense—especially not the notion that her momma and Thorton had actually married, that she wasn't illegitimate after all, that Thorton and Ava had lived as husband and wife and then divorced somewhere down the line. That was crazy! Why wouldn't Ava have told her about Thorton if that had happened?

Unable to fathom a reasonable answer, Rachel reached an obvious conclusion. Thorton had paid someone to forge a marriage license. A man of his means could do that easily enough. Convinced she had it figured out, she handed the certificate back to him.

"Nice try," she said. "Had me going there for a second."

Thorton's eyebrows met in the middle. "I don't understand," he said.

"You made a fake license," she explained. "Nice job too,

state seal, notary public, everything. Real professional." She leaned back, pleased with her instincts.

For a second, Thorton remained speechless. Then he laid the license on the desk and found his voice. "You're a real pistol," he said. "Smart as a whip and pretty as anything. But you're far too cynical for a woman of your young years."

Rachel shrugged. His words meant nothing to her.

"I married your mother," he said. "That license is genuine."

"Yeah and I've got some prime beach front property out in Death Valley to sell you," she said. "I can guarantee you a real deal on it."

Thorton rubbed his face with both hands, forehead to cheeks to chin, forehead to cheeks to chin. When finished, he focused on Rachel again. "What I'm telling you is true," he said. "I can get someone from the courthouse to verify the validity of the license."

Rachel smiled. The game seemed almost fun now that she had figured it out. "I'm sure you can," she said. "What with you a former mayor and all."

Thorton picked up the license again, studied it. "Your grandfather hated me," he said softly.

"Grandfather hated everybody," said Rachel. "Especially when he was drinking."

"Which was most of the time."

Rachel smiled sadly at the truth of Thorton's words.

"Things at home were awful for Ava," he continued. "Harder than anything most people ever have to face. The verbal abuse, the emotional tyranny. Theodore Wilson was meaner than a rabid dog when he got worked up."

Rachel rubbed her hands together. Ava never talked about

these kinds of things.

"Ava and I loved each other," said Thorton. "We wanted to marry, but Ava was only seventeen."

"I thought you said you did marry."

Thorton nodded. "I did. We wanted to do it the right way, church and all, with her mom and dad's blessings. But Theodore would have no part of it. Said his daughter would not marry one such as me. My daddy worked down at the mill, you know. Not the place that respectable people went to look to find a match for their children."

"But they weren't rich," argued Rachel. "Granddad Wilson never held a job that anybody could tell. And he went through money like a stove burning wood."

"But his family had some money in earlier times," said Thorton. "Depression took some of it. Wilson drank up most of the rest."

"And you lived on the wrong side of the tracks," said Rachel, going along with the story.

"We couldn't even see the tracks," said Thorton. "Times were hard." He looked at the license once more. "The Christmas after Ava's friend died in the accident, we decided to run off and marry. Ava had taken all she could. Didn't want to wait another minute, much less until she turned eighteen the next October."

"So you and Momma eloped?" Rachel didn't even try to hide her disbelief. "You were married when I was born? How did you hide that from everybody, explain that to me?"

Thorton laid the license down, walked around and sat on the edge of the desk, crossing his ankles. "I know this will sound crazy," he said. "But we were married for just one day.

One day and one night."

Rachel squeezed the arms of her chair. This made no sense! But then nothing had made sense since Mother's Day. "You've got my attention," she said.

"Her daddy found out the night we ran off," he explained. "He scared Ava's Momma into telling him where we were."

"Ava's Momma?"

"Yeah, she beat all you ever saw when matters got down to brass tacks. She's the one who signed for us to marry. Ava was just seventeen, remember? But Mrs. Wilson went with us to the justice of the peace over in Asheville, signed her name pretty as you please. Guess you didn't see that on the license."

Rachel shook her head. She hadn't bothered to read the names on the bottom of the certificate. "You say Wilson scared her?"

"Yeah, Mrs. Wilson told me later that she drove home after the marriage and fixed Theodore's supper. At the table he started asking where Ava was, why she wasn't home. Gertrude stalled for a long time. Told him Ava was with a friend. I don't know how she planned to keep the marriage a secret for too long. I guess she didn't think that far ahead. But anyway . . . Theodore wouldn't let it go. He started stomping around, wanting to know which friend Ava had gone to see."

Thorton moved back to the seat behind the desk. "Mrs. Wilson told me later she tried to get him drunk so he would pass out and leave her alone. But it didn't work. Sometime after midnight, he took to threatening her. Pulled his belt off and started slapping the air around her head. Didn't hit her she said, but frightened her pretty badly. He said if she didn't tell him where Rachel was, she would live to regret it the rest of her life. By daybreak he had worn her down."

"So she told?"

Thorton nodded. "She figured Theodore would leave us alone since we had been together for the night and all. Thought he would give up and let us go on with our lives."

"But he didn't?"

"Nope."

Rachel saw Thorton's mouth sagging into a frown. He looked like he wanted to cry.

"What happened?" she asked, not sure she believed Thorton, but unable to leave the rest of his tale untold.

"Theodore woke us an hour or so after daylight the next morning. We were at a little motel outside of Asheville. He brought two drinking buddies with him. Pulled Ava right out of the room, took her away from me."

"You didn't fight him?"

Thorton's eyes watered but he gathered himself before any tears fell. "What could I do?" he asked. "He broke in on us while we were asleep. And his friends had pistols. Before I could do anything, Theodore had jerked Ava out of bed and hauled her out the door. I ran after them, but I didn't have on any shoes, and then . . . then they were gone."

Rachel tried to determine what she believed about the story. Could it be true? Thorton sounded sincere, but he could have made it all up. But why would he do that? Simple. He had a reputation to protect, and she threatened it if she went public. With this story though, Thorton could maintain his squeaky-clean image.

"You didn't try to re-claim your wife?" she asked, deciding to test him further. "You gave her up that easily?"

For the first time since she met him, she saw a hint of frustration in Thorton. His hands clenched and unclenched. "You're tough, aren't you." he stated.

"I have to be," she said. "Illegitimate child and all that."

"But I'm telling you that you aren't illegitimate," he said. "You still don't believe me?"

"I don't know what to believe," she said. "A lot of crazy things have happened to me lately, a lot to soak in, you know what I mean?"

Thorton rubbed his face. "I don't know what else I can do," he said. "Except to say I'm telling you the truth."

"So you let Ava go," said Rachel, not backing away from the accusation. "Got a quick divorce. Maybe you could show me the divorce papers. That would prove your case. Unless of course, Theodore Wilson kept those and you don't have a copy."

"We never divorced," said Thorton. "Wilson had the marriage annulled the next day."

Rachel mulled that over and suddenly realized its implication. "You're telling me that Momma got pregnant that first night?"

Thorton nodded.

"And that her father had the marriage annulled before he knew her condition?"

Another nod from Thorton. Rachel found it hard to breathe.

"By the time she knew she was pregnant it was too late for us to re-marry and make it proper," Thorton said. "Not that I think Wilson would have let us marry anyway. I have no doubt that the man preferred for Ava to have a child out of wedlock than for her to marry a man he didn't approve."

"So what happened next?"

"Theodore sent Ava to Missouri to live with his sister and have the baby."

"Which turned out to be me."

"You got it. She lived there for several years."

"You didn't know where she was?"

"Nope. I didn't even know she was pregnant. Nobody told me anything, not even Gertrude. Wilson had scared her so bad the night Ava and I married that she wouldn't speak to me again. I figured he had sent Ava away to keep her from me. Truth is, it was some of both. He sent her away to keep her from me **and** to prevent the neighbors from thinking he had a wayward daughter."

"And by the time she moved back . . ." Rachel's voice trailed away as she answered her question in her head.

"I had already married Louise," said Thorton, his eyes moist again. "I wanted to find Ava, wanted to wait . . . but she was gone and I didn't know if she would ever come back. But that's what happened, you have to believe it. Ava would never have slept with a man before marriage, no matter how much she loved him. You ought to know that better than anybody."

It seemed to Rachel that all the air had seeped out of the room. She didn't know what to believe. Thorton's story sounded plausible. But could she accept it? If so, what happened next? Did any of this matter, true or not?

Thorton reached into his desk and pulled out another manila envelope. Rachel wondered what other surprise he could spring. He opened the envelope and pulled something out and handed it across the desk to her.

"It's a picture of me and Ava," he explained." I was a lot thinner back then."

Rachel took the framed, five by seven black and white photo without responding to his attempt at humor. Her face blanched white. She rubbed the glass frame as if trying to wipe away the images under it. But she couldn't. The man and woman in the frame continued to smile at each other, their eyes glowing. Thorton wore a dark suit and a thin black tie and white shirt. His hair was dark then, as black as asphalt and so shiny with oil it looked like someone had emptied a tube of hair cream on his head. Ava looked beautiful, her face thin as always but not hollow like it was now. She had on white gloves and a trim dress, light in color. She gazed at Thorton in the picture, obviously in love.

"It's you and Momma," Rachel said.

"I knew you were smart," said Thorton.

Rachel ignored his remark. Something in the picture bothered her, something she couldn't quite identify. It seemed familiar somehow, like she had dreamed it in one of the few moments she had actually slept in the last month. The picture unnerved her in a mysterious way.

"When was it taken?" she asked.

"On the day we married," he said.

Rachel had already guessed his answer. But something in her still refused to accept what Thorton kept pressing on her—that instead of being illegitimate, her life had originated from a one-day marriage between two people who loved each other. But why? Why couldn't she just accept what he said?

She was angry, that's why—angry at Thorton for leaving it up to her to seek him out. Wasn't that proof he really didn't care for her at all? If she hadn't gone searching for him, she still wouldn't know who her father was!

Another notion flared up. Maybe her refusal to trust Thorton went deeper than that. Maybe she didn't want to believe him because if she did, she would have to reshape her own self-image. To give up her present identity as a bastard child meant she had to release her anger, had to open her hands and let the rage run out of her fingers like water through an open grate. To accept what Thorton said would force her to reform her whole view of life. After all, a child with loving parents has less to prove than one who doesn't—less to overcome. If Thorton and Ava had married, if even for a night, then "Rush It Rachel" would need to re-examine herself, the things that made her tick. She would have to reconsider what she saw as important. She would need to consider the possibility of slowing down some, paying more attention to becoming someone rather than achieving something.

The idea scared Rachel more than she wanted to admit. Right now she knew who she was, even if it wasn't always easy. She knew how to act as "Rush It Rachel." To become a new person required a lot of energy, and she didn't know if she had what it took to do that.

"Okay," she said. "I admit that you and Momma were sweethearts. But this picture doesn't prove anything more than that."

"But I showed you the marriage license," Thorton pressed.

"Like I said, someone could have forged that for you," Rachel argued.

Thorton sighed with exasperation. "You don't want to believe me," he said. "For reasons I can't understand."

"Momma didn't put your name on my birth certificate," she said. "So why should I believe you were married?"

Thorton shrugged. "I can't make you trust me," he said. "But everything I've told you is true."

Maybe so, thought Rachel. But somehow, she wasn't convinced. Ava had kept Thorton's name a secret all these years. Maybe she had good reason. Maybe she knew something that made him unacceptable as a father, made her shy away from him after Rachel's birth.

"Why didn't Momma tell me about you?" she asked, deciding to follow out the line of thinking.

"Same reason she wouldn't tell everybody else. She thought it better to keep things as they were. She and Ray were married, as were Gertrude and I. All of us knew. Like I said earlier, I wanted her to tell, at least tell you. But she had already lived through the shame of it all. So she always refused. Didn't want to upset our lives."

"That was noble of her." Rachel felt a twinge of anger at Ava. No matter how good Ava's motives, she shouldn't have kept Thorton's name a secret.

"Ava tried to protect us all," said Thorton. "But she should have told you. Guess she figured that out too late."

Rachel rubbed the photo again. Thorton was right about Ava. She tried to protect everyone. That's why she never told.

"After Ray's death, she couldn't deal with any more emotional upheaval," Rachel said. "And after awhile I let it drop. Then the Alzheimer's invaded."

Thorton took a breath. "I don't know if it was right or wrong to keep it a secret all these years," he said. "Better or worse for any of us. Though I've always wanted to know you, it scared me too. I have to be honest about that."

Rachel heard sincerity in his voice. But so many years had

passed. How could she accept this now? How could she embrace the notion that she had a father, a man that loved her even though she hadn't met him until some days ago? She glanced at the picture again.

Was Thorton right? Was this the way God sometimes worked? In the shadows, watching over us even when we don't know it? Providing for us? Always near to help when we need it most?

She remembered the song, "His eye is on the sparrow, and I know he watches me." It sounded so good, so comforting.

But could she believe all this? Throw up her hands and accept David Thorton? Start over with her image of herself? Wipe out the self-portrait she had taken forty-two years to develop and start a new one?

She put her head in her hands. It was too hard, too painful. No. She couldn't do it yet. She needed some final proof of Thorton's story, some sign that God was truly in this, some way to finally determine Thorton's trustworthiness. Tears pushed to her eyes, but she angrily brushed them away.

She glanced again at the picture of Ava and Thorton. Ava seemed so happy in the picture. "Tell me, Momma," she whispered. "Tell me if all this is true?"

Ava smiled at Thorton behind the frame. She seemed so joyful, exactly as a young woman should look on the arm of her new husband. She was so pretty too, her hair wavy, her white gloves so chic and sophisticated, her dress so neat and snug on her petite figure.

Rachel felt her breath catch. The color drained from her face. She stared at the picture as if she could make Ava speak through the frame if she studied it hard enough.

Thorton eased up from his chair. "You okay?" he asked.

"The dress!"

"What?"

"That's what bothered me about this picture."

"It's the dress she wore when we married," said Thorton.

"But you don't understand!" said Rachel. "I saw it . . . saw it when I packed Momma up a month ago. She . . . she put it on when I left the room to answer the phone!"

Thorton caught his breath, but Rachel didn't look up. The dress on Ava in the picture was the wrinkled linen dress she found in the bottom of the chest on Mother's Day! Ava wore that dress the day she married David Thorton!

The tears falling freely now, Rachel threw back her head and laughed. Ava had awakened from her Alzheimer's long enough to give her a sign that she had been loved by two fathers. The wedding dress in her lap had overshadowed the one on her body. But she had put on the linen one on Mother's Day, the day she told Rachel her father's name. That fact, plus this picture, proved to Rachel beyond any doubt that Ava had loved David Thorton and wanted her to love him too.

Her legs trembling, Rachel stood and moved to Thorton. She had received her sign. The wedding dress proved it. And God is there close by, even though you don't always see the holy presence. God provides, even though you don't always recognize it when it happens.

Thorton opened his arms. Rachel stopped for a second, her eyes wet, her heart thumping hard. Could she do this? Could she accept this man? And herself as well?

"I'm your father," said Thorton. "I've loved you since the day I knew you existed."

Rachel smiled. Her father loved her. Just like God.

In that instant, she realized she believed him. Her heart soared. If this father loved her, then perhaps anything was possible, anything at all.

She hugged David Thorton. It felt like heaven. ❧

MONDAY

ONE MONTH LATER

Rachel wiped her hands on her apron, took a step away from the table and moved to her momma sitting by the open kitchen window. A slight breeze drifted through the window screen, and a cardinal so red it looked like a fresh apple fluttered in and out of a bird feeder just off the back porch. At Ava's side, Rachel pulled back a strand of hair that had fallen in Ava's eyes.

"You okay, Momma?" she asked.

Ava stared at the cardinal.

Rachel smiled. Ava loved watching the birds at the feeder, and right after breakfast every morning, Rachel led her to the rocker so she could see them. The cardinal pecked at the grainy food for several seconds and then darted into the oak tree by the garage. Rachel pulled Ava's shawl up around her shoulders. Moving her from the nursing home hadn't done a thing to warm her up.

"You need a blanket?" Rachel asked. "I washed your blue one last night."

Ava stared at the cardinal.

"Hang on a second," said Rachel. "I'll go get one."

It took less than a minute to reach Ava's bedroom and open the closet. The blanket lay on the top shelf. On her tiptoes,

Rachel pulled down the blanket and turned to go back to the kitchen. But then she pivoted and stepped into the closet again. Her eyes landed on the two garment bags hanging inside. For an instant, she stood still as a fence post. Then, ever so gently, she lifted her right hand and touched the garment bag nearest to her. She knew what the bag held—the dress Ava wore the day she married David Thorton. Rachel had found it in the clothes closet at her church the Monday after Father's Day. Relieved, she quickly re-claimed it and carried it to the dry cleaners. After picking it up on Friday, she had placed it in Ava's closet alongside her other wedding dress.

As she had done every morning since retrieving it from the cleaners, Rachel now unzipped the garment bag and ran her fingers over the front of the dress. She still couldn't believe all she had done in the last four weeks. Like introducing David Thorton to Tim, and talking with both of them about how and when Thorton should meet Kara. She had also met Thorton's wife and talked with the two of them about how and when to meet his kids and grandchildren. Next, she had taken Thorton to see Ava. Though Ava didn't recognize him, Rachel could tell from the expression on Thorton's face that he had needed to see her. What a week that was!

She had started eating and sleeping again too. Her face had filled out again and her eyes had some sparkle back in them. Pleased, Rachel focused again on the present moment, zipped up the garment bag, and walked to Ava's window. The place felt holy to her now, a spot on the hardwood floor where God's feet had touched down.

She eased into the rocker in the exact same place where Ava had awakened. Now the sun washed in the window and warmed her face. It felt good. She closed her eyes and remembered the other events of the past month, the things she had managed to do with God's grace and Tim's gentle love . . .

She and Tim had sipped coffee and talked into the wee hours the night of Father's Day. As always, Tim mostly listened as Rachel poured out the story Thorton had told her. When she finished she confided to Tim that she believed Thorton. Something had switched over in her—the meeting with Thorton had swirled her around deep inside. It had changed her, she said, shaped her in ways she couldn't really explain just yet. But she thought it was for the better, though that too would need some time to prove. Now, she said, taking Tim's hand and squeezing it, she had come to the point where she wanted some new direction in life.

"What kind of direction?" asked Tim, a touch of anxiety in his voice.

Rachel kissed his hand and smiled. "Not to worry," she said. "Nothing about us. Fact is, I'm more in love with you than ever. You've treated me so well through all this, been so patient."

Tim hung his head, embarrassed at such a compliment. "Then what?" he asked. "What kind of changes?"

"I want to take care of Momma," she said.

Tim cleared his throat. "What about your work?"

"I want to work less." There, she had said it.

Tim laid her hand on the table and picked up his coffee cup. "You sure about that?"

Rachel took a deep breath. "I've thought about this for a long time," she said. "Wanted to do it, but didn't think I could—didn't feel I could risk it. But now I believe I can. I

want to make your coffee for you every morning, want to walk
Kara to the school bus. I want to make sure that whatever time
Momma has left, I'm here to share it."

Tim studied his coffee for several seconds. "You said, 'work
less'" he finally said. "What's your notion?"

"I can take care of Momma in the morning," Rachel said.
"Mrs. Becker will come for the afternoon. I've already checked
with her about the possibility. She said she could do it now
that her oldest has moved out."

"I come home by five most days," Tim said. "I can do my
part too."

Rachel wanted to hug him. "I'll join you by six or so," she
said. "Leave those late afternoon appointments to somebody
younger."

"Yeah, you are getting up in years," Tim smiled.

Rachel grinned. Silence came to the room for a minute.
Then Tim said. "Our house is mighty small for Ava."

Rachel nodded. "I've thought of that too. We can take
Momma's house off the market, sell our place, and move in
there. Use the money from our sale to pay Mrs. Becker."

"If we all do our part, we might just swing it," said Tim.

And so they had reached the decisions that altered their lives
forever. Rachel told her partner at Blue Ridge Real Estate to
hire a new agent to replace the hours she would no longer
work. She pulled up the "For Sale" sign in the front yard of
Ava's house. Agreed on a salary for Mrs. Becker. Packed Ava up
and moved her back into her old room. Found the wedding
dress at the church clothes closet, cleaned it and placed it
beside the more formal dress. And she actually started living a
less hurried life . . .

The sound of a phone startled Rachel out of her memories. Up from the chair, she moved to the front of the house. Her steps felt light, her shoulders relaxed. She knew she had some hard days to come. Ava's condition would only worsen from this point on. She would not live much longer. But she would not spend her last days alone.

Rachel picked up the phone.

"It's me," said Tim. "What are you doing?"

"Watching television and eating bon bons," she lied. "What else do I have to do?"

"Funny woman," he said. "Mrs. Becker comes in at twelve, right?"

"Right."

"I'm not real busy today," he said. "What if I take the afternoon off, pick you up and we go hiking up by Crystal Lake?"

Rachel squeezed the phone. She had an appointment at three and enough paper work to choke a horse. She opened her mouth to say 'no' but the word refused to come out. "I'll make a picnic," she said instead. "Egg salad sandwiches okay?"

"And some bon bons," said Tim.

"I ate them all," she said.

"See you at noon," laughed Tim.

A wide smile on her face, Rachel hung up the phone. She was still a working woman. Nothing would change that. But she was a wife first—and a Momma and a daughter. From now on, she wouldn't let anything change that either. ❧